I AM CANADA

GRAVES OF ICE

The Lost Franklin Expedition

by John Wilson

Scholastic Canada Ltd.

Toronto New York London Auckland Sydney
Mexico City New Delhi Hong Kong Buenos Aires

Copyright © 2014 by John Wilson. All rights reserved.

A Dear Canada Book. Published by Scholastic Canada Ltd.
SCHOLASTIC and I AM CANADA and logos are trademarks
and/or registered trademarks of Scholastic Inc.

www.scholastic.ca

Library and Archives Canada Cataloguing in Publication

Wilson, John (John Alexander), 1951-, author
Graves of ice : the lost Franklin expedition / by John Wilson.

(I am Canada)
Issued in print and electronic formats.
ISBN 978-1-4431-0794-5 (bound).--ISBN 978-1-4431-2896-4 (html)

1. Franklin, John, Sir, 1786-1847--Juvenile fiction. 2. Northwest
Passage--Juvenile fiction. 3. Arctic regions--Discovery and exploration--
Juvenile fiction. I. Title. II. Series: I am Canada

PS8595.I5834G74 2014   jC813'.54   C2013-905342-5
                   C2013-905434-3

No part of this publication may be reproduced or stored in a retrieval
system, or transmitted in any form or by any means, electronic,
mechanical, recording, or otherwise, without written permission of the
publisher, Scholastic Canada Ltd., 604 King Street West, Toronto, Ontario
M5V 1E1, Canada. In the case of photocopying or other reprographic
copying, a licence must be obtained from Access Copyright
(Canadian Copyright Licensing Agency), 1 Yonge Street, Suite 800,
Toronto, Ontario M5E 1E5 (1-800-893-5777).

6 5 4 3 2 1   Printed in Canada 114   14 15 16 17 18

The display type was set in Berkeley.

First printing January 2014

*For the real George William Chambers
and his 128 lost comrades.*

Research for this novel was generously supported by
a grant from the Access Copyright Foundation.

Prologue

I place the final flat stone on the low mound before me and stand up. It's not much of a grave, but it's all I can manage. Sickness and starvation have left me too weak to do more than scrabble out a shallow hollow in the frozen ground and scrape a few stones over the body — enough, I hope, to keep the curious foxes away.

I should say something over this final grave. There have been many in my life — my brother's, Simon's, John Torrington's, William Braine's, Sir John's, Lieutenant Irving's, Davy's — they all had someone to speak for them.

"Here lies the body of Commander James Fitzjames," I begin. "He was born . . . "

When was Mr. Fitzjames born? If I ever knew, it's gone from my tired brain now.

"He died today, September . . . "

What's today's date? It's September 1849, but the day hasn't mattered for a long time. Only the seasons matter now — the cold terrifying darkness

1

of winter or the bright hopeful light of summer.

"I've done the best I can, Mr. Fitzjames. Strange, but after five years together and all we've been through, I still can't call you James. You are an officer; I am a cabin boy. That will never change.

"Do you remember when we first met? It was on the Woolwich dock in April of 1845. You stood at the bottom of the gangway leading up to Erebus's deck, surrounded by the mad activity of preparing the ship for her great journey. You scared me, looking so grand in your formal uniform, but your smile and a few kind words calmed the nerves of a frightened boy.

"We've been through so much together since those far-off days in a different world. We've seen triumphs and tragedies enough for the pen of Mr. Shakespeare or Mr. Dickens — but who will ever know?"

A wracking cough drives me to my knees, leaving me gasping for air, my body heaving in spasms of pain. As the fit passes, I rock back onto my haunches and stare at the fine spray of blood spattering the patch of dirty snow in front of me. "It will not be long until I join you," I croak. "But who will dig my grave?"

I struggle to my feet, wipe my mouth and manage a shaky salute, remembering to keep my palm down, the Navy way. "I'm sorry. I should not salute when

I am not wearing a cap. I have learned enough to know that is unforgivable.

"If only it had turned out differently. It's a shame that so much hope and promise came to this. Nonetheless, it has been a pleasure to serve with you, Mr. Fitzjames."

I can think of nothing else to say. My gaze drifts over the few pitiful possessions that we have managed to drag this far — the tiny canvas awning that is all we have for shelter, a sleeping sack made from two blankets sewn together, a musket, a tin cup and a flint, although there is no wood left to burn. Mr. Fitzjames's wonderful brass telescope lies buried with him. It is no use to me — my salvation will depend on someone seeing me, not the other way around.

I turn my back on the grave and stumble across the stream, past the scavenged carcass of the deer and up the low hill that is our lookout point. It's a gentle slope, but walking is difficult. It is something I have done without thinking most of my life, but now I must focus on placing one numbed foot before the other. Left foot, right foot, left foot, right foot — a mesmerizing, shuffling rhythm. The soles of my rotting boots flap mournfully with each step and give flashing glimpses of my black, frostbitten toes. Likely very few can be saved even if I am rescued.

Another fit of coughing wracks me as I reach the hilltop, stagger over to a flat rock and sit down. The hills behind me are patched with snow, the dark rocky shore barren and lifeless, the swelling water stretching away to the far horizon where ice floes glisten in the low sun. My gaze rests on the sharp, unbroken line between the sea and sky. It is late in the season, but if there are still search vessels or whaling ships nearby, that is where they will come from.

There are no more choices. I am too weak to seek help, so it must find me. My joints ache, my gums bleed and my teeth are loose — signs of scurvy. The remains of the deer might keep me alive for a few more days, but what the animals have left will rot fast and there is nothing else.

The coming cold and the ache of starvation scare me, but not as much as the loneliness — the horrifying, empty, crushing loneliness. I am George William Chambers, the last of Sir John Franklin's mighty expedition that left England with such high hopes and dreams more than four years ago.

We were to find the Northwest Passage and return home heroes. How has it come to this?

My mind is wandering into the past more and more these days. Sometimes I barely know what is real and what is only a vivid memory. The ghosts of my past — my family, Fitzjames, Franklin, Crozier, and most of all Davy — haunt my dreams and, increasingly, my waking hours as well. Is that what death is? A release from the present, a letting go of reality, a long slow drift into an endless past?

Memories flood over me — scenes, images, incidents — but all so real that I must fight to prevent them from overwhelming me. Should I struggle against the past, force myself to stay in the present and continue searching for that glimmer of hope on the horizon? Just one whaling ship and all would be changed . . .

Seductive voices and images fill my head. Am I going mad? The past, my story, is pulling me back, away from my unhappy present, back to a time when all the dead were alive, back to the beginning.

Chapter 1
Beginnings
Woolwich, England, 1834–1844

From my attic window in the narrow red-brick house at 58 Church Hill, Woolwich, I could look out over the dockyards and the eternal bustle on the Thames River. Ships of all shapes and sizes came and went from distant, exotic lands and fuelled the dreams that were my escape from the crowded house I shared with my parents, four sisters and three brothers.

In the evenings we would congregate in the main floor parlour, my father reading to us or telling stories, my mother sewing. That was when I first heard of the strange realms of Canada and of Sir John Franklin. Father used to read from his book: *Narrative of a Journey to the Shores of the Polar Sea, in the Years 1819, 20, 21, and 22.*

My mother did not completely approve of Father's subject matter, but, at six and seven years old, I was captivated by the tinted plates of the land, animals and peoples of those wilds. Haunting names like Slave Lake and Bloody Falls excited me. Even more, the tales of starvation, murder and heroic rescue fed my imagination as I lay awake in my bed at night. Franklin — The Man Who Ate His Boots, as he was known — was my childhood hero. Despite the deaths and suffering, I saw his first expedition only as a magnificent adventure.

My father also told us stories of his own younger days as a Royal Marine in the wars against Napoleon. His careworn face would light up with a ready smile when my brothers and I begged for tales of adventure. We sat at his feet, warmed by the crackling fire in the narrow grate, as he filled his pipe and pretended not to heed our pleadings.

"Tell us the tale of the *Billy Ruffian*," I urged.

"Yes, please," Alexander and William, my younger brothers, agreed. Thomas didn't join in. He sat to one side, silent but listening intently to every word.

"Perhaps I could prevail upon your mother to enlighten us on the complexities of needlework or sewing," Father suggested. It was a game we played — Father suggesting stories we had no interest in until we were at fever pitch for the exciting one we all knew he would tell.

"No!" we shouted as one voice. "*Billy Ruffian. Billy Ruffian.*"

"Very well then. If you're certain."

"We are! We are!"

"Back in those dark days, when it seemed that the demon Napoleon Bonaparte would rule the world, the only thing standing between him and an invasion of these isles was His Majesty's Royal Navy." We cheered and Father settled deeper into his chair.

"I was a mere boy in 1805, the youngest Royal Marine in the squadron," Father continued. "I was nervous and worried that I would not be able to learn all the complex duties I would be expected to undertake, but I was thrilled to be assigned to HMS *Bellerophon*. Can anyone tell me what the sailors called the *Bellerophon*?" Father asked with a smile.

"*Billy Ruffian*," Alexander and William shouted.

"And who was Bellerophon?"

"The warrior who rode the winged horse Pegasus and defeated the Chimera," I answered.

"Well done, George. I am glad you pay attention to your lessons. Now, as you know, at the Battle of Trafalgar, the French and Spanish fleets greatly outgunned Admiral Nelson's squadron, but our famous admiral had a trick up his sleeve. Instead of sailing alongside the enemy and exchanging fire as everyone else had done until then, he determined to cut the French line in two places and destroy their ships piecemeal.

"The *Billy Ruffian* was to the fore when we broke through the enemy line and became engaged with the seventy-four–gun French warship *Aigle*. Our rigging became entangled, and for an hour or more we were locked together so close that our gunners could thrust their bayonets into the bodies of the enemy sailors through the *Aigle*'s gun ports.

"The French had the habit in battle of placing sharpshooters in the rigging of their vessels — "

"That is how Lord Nelson was slain on HMS *Victory*," I interrupted, eager to show off my knowledge.

"Indeed," Father said, leaning down to ruffle my hair. "He fell in the moment of his greatest success, shot through the breast by a French sharpshooter. Our own Captain Cooke on the *Billy Ruffian* also fell in exactly that way. In fact, the musket fire from the *Aigle*'s rigging swept our decks with such murderous intensity that the scuppers ran red with blood.

"And at that very moment, the French marines attempted to storm over *Billy Ruffian*'s rail. Now was my chance to be involved, since it was the Royal Marines' job to repulse these attacks. I was scared, I admit it freely, but if everyone else was performing their duty, how could I not?

"I rushed forward with my companions and found myself close to a huge Frenchman who had leaped the narrow gap between the vessels and was charging a young midshipman on the quarterdeck. The man was immense."

"How big was he?" we shrieked. This was also part of our game. We asked, and with each telling the man grew in stature.

"Well," Father said, scratching his chin. "It was hard to tell in the heat of battle, but he must have been close to eight feet tall."

We gasped in mock wonder.

"I was too far off to reach this giant before he would decapitate the poor midshipman with his cutlass, so I shouted the one French word I knew."

"*Arrêtez!*" we yelled at the top of our lungs.

"Exactly," Father continued. "I yelled, *Arrêtez*, and it was just enough to cause the man to hesitate. I leaped forward and thrust the long bayonet on the end of my trusty Brown Bess musket — which was longer by a good few inches than I was tall — into the Frenchman's side. He fell, but as he did so, he swept his cutlass wide, catching me a glancing blow on the side of the head."

"Show us the scar," we shouted.

With theatrical slowness, Father lifted the hair

on the right side of his head to reveal a long, livid line across his scalp. "After the fight," he said once his hair was back in place, "while I was having my head bandaged, the young midshipman, the only man unwounded on the quarterdeck that day, visited me to thank me for saving his life."

"Who was he?"

"He introduced himself as John Franklin of Spilsby, Lincolnshire, and promised to help me if it was ever in his power to do so. Now he is Sir John Franklin, famous explorer and The Man Who Ate His Boots."

"Read us some of his book," we pleaded.

"I think," our mother said from the doorway, "that will be enough excitement for the boys tonight."

We groaned and complained, but half-heartedly, before we trudged up the stairs to bed, our heads filled with adventures and battles.

Quiet though my brother Thomas was, Father's stories bewitched him even more than I. He left us for a life on the sea as soon as he was able. Tragically, after less than one year away, he was lost when his ship foundered in a storm in the Channel. His body, and those of many others of the crew, washed ashore near Portsmouth and was returned home for burial in the local churchyard. On the day of his funeral, I stood by his open grave, overwhelmed as much by the display of emotion from the black-clad adults as by my own confused thoughts. How could Thomas's adventure end so quickly and so sadly? It wasn't fair.

After Thomas was put to rest, I took employment as a junior clerk for the princely sum of nine shillings a week. I worked for Mr. Mumford, a decent man who ran a company supplying wares to the Navy.

It was tedious work, bent over a cramped desk in a tiny room beneath a grubby window, but my workplace was at the very water's edge, so I could occasionally escape to walk by the docks, listening to the shouts and songs of the sailors, the rattle and clang of chains and the lap of the tide against hulls.

One day I was sitting in my favourite spot on a bollard, looking out over the reeking mud flats at a newly arrived vessel whose three masts and single line of eighteen cannons down each side marked her as a fast frigate. The crew were busy painting the upper woodwork and setting the running rigging.

A voice from over the edge of the dock startled me. "Ain't you going to give me a hand up?"

I looked down to see a filthy face staring up

at me. A mop of dirty red hair framed the face, which wore a broad smile.

"Well, you going to sit there gawking, or help?"

"Sorry," I mumbled, sliding off the bollard and reaching over the edge of the dock. The creature I hauled up seemed, from the neck down, to be made from the thick, grey slime of the river bottom, and smelled as if it had been dead a long time.

"Thank you kindly," the boy said, scraping the worst of the slime off himself. "I don't smell the best, do I?" he added with a lopsided smile. He was shorter than me and slightly built, and he wore nothing but a pair of short trousers with a filthy bag tied at his waist.

"What were you doing?" I asked. "Did you fall in?"

The boy's grin exposed a row of uneven teeth. "Ain't you never heard of mud-larking?"

"Of course, I have," I shot back, not wanting to seem stupid. "It's treasure hunting when the tide's out."

"Don't know that it's treasure hunting, though I did hear of a lad once found a diamond ring. I expect it's just a story though. Pickings're better in the city — best stuff's gone by the time it's washed down this far. Still, I ain't wasted my morning." The boy untied the neck of his sack and shook the contents out onto the cobbles.

The pile looked like things my family might throw away, but the boy sorted through it eagerly. "A few rags that'll wash up good enough" — he lifted some unidentifiable pieces and what looked like a silk kerchief and set them aside. "Might get a penny for this" — he turned a battered pewter tankard over. "Still holds ale, I'll warrant." He placed it on the rags, lifted the final piece, spat on it and cleaned as much mud as possible off it. It looked like a coin, round and quite large. He hefted it in his palm. "Thought it was a silver crown when I first seen it, but it's only some old soldier's medal. Still, might be worth something at the pawn."

The boy replaced the items in his sack and held out his hand. "Name's David Young," he said, "but everyone calls me Davy. Much obliged for the hand up."

"George Chambers," I said, clasping his grubby paw. "You're welcome."

Davy tilted his head and looked at me. "You from round here?" he asked.

"Yes," I replied. "I live on Church Hill, number 58."

"Bit of a toff, then," Davy said.

"No," I said, offended by the idea that Davy thought I was an upper-class snob. "I work as a

14

clerk for Mr. Mumford." I pointed to the nearby warehouse where I had my desk.

"Like I said, a toff what can read and write."

I had nothing to say to this. I was proud of my reading and writing.

"Don't look so offended, Georgie. I meant nothing by it. I like you. Maybe we'll have some adventures together one of these days."

Swinging his sack over his shoulder, Davy strolled off along the dock, whistling a music hall tune. After a few steps he stopped, looked back over his shoulder and said, "I ain't going to be mud-larking forever, you know. I got plans. Maybe I'll take you along with me on my journey to fame and fortune." With a broad wink, he turned back and continued down the dock.

I watched until he was out of sight, fascinated by his vulgar confidence. My mother would have been shocked that I had even talked with a mud-lark, but there was something about Davy — his confidence, jaunty manner and knowledge — that I found interesting. And his talk of adventure. Adventure's what I craved more than anything else.

Chapter 2
Resurrection
Woolwich, England, 1844

I never thought I would see Davy again but, to my surprise, there he was standing by my favourite bollard only three days after I had helped him from the river. With great enthusiasm, he told me how much he had made from selling the rags and trinkets he'd saved from the mud. Even though it was mere pennies, his enthusiasm was infectious and I found myself being drawn into his world, so different from the one I knew.

We saw each other frequently, and eventually took to meeting daily by the river. I began sharing my lunch with him and telling him stories of Father's life in Nelson's navy. Davy made me repeat his favourite tales endlessly. I suspect that with those tales I planted a seed in his mind.

In exchange, Davy regaled me with stories of the underside of life in the city I thought I knew. He and many others had no secure home and lived by scrounging and stealing whatever they could. I was shocked, but I was also fascinated, and if I was honest with myself, attracted. Davy's life was hard and he lived on the edges of the law, but he was free. In comparison to my life, which I was increasingly seeing as a prison with me chained to my clerk's desk, Davy could come and go as he chose, with no responsibilities and beholden to no one. I began to envy him.

By the river we talked of wild, unlikely schemes for getting rich quickly, or impossible plans for escape to exotic, unreachable places like India or Canada. Davy, in particular, was full of ideas for bettering his life.

One day he told me that a plan was coming to fruition and that I had to help him. I agreed without thinking. Davy told me to sneak out of the house and meet him by the river after my family were asleep. Once more I agreed. It was only after I returned to my desk that I began to worry about what I was getting into, but I was committed. I could not let my friend down.

That night, nervous and excited, I dressed, crept downstairs and made my way to the docks. Davy was waiting.

"Hey there, Georgie," he said when he saw me. "You ready for an adventure?"

The moon was almost full and cast a silvery glow on the river. I could see Davy quite clearly.

His teeth gleamed in the light as he grinned at me.

"I'm not sure," I said.

The grin vanished. "You ain't sure? But you're here."

"I promised I'd come, but I'm scared. I don't want to get into trouble. Mother and Father would be horrified if they knew I was here."

To my surprise, Davy laughed out loud. "Mother and father," he said. He calmed down and looked straight at me. "When were you born?" he asked.

Confused by the sudden change of topic, I said, "September 5th, 1827."

"Maybe I was, too. It were about then. What does your da look like?"

"Ordinary," I said, still confused. "Grey hair and whiskers, wrinkled face, but smiling eyes."

"My da had a big nose. I only know that because I have one and me ma's nose were small, so I must have got it from him. I never knew him."

"Did he die when you were young?"

Davy laughed again, bitter this time. "For all I know, he's still alive. Might even be drinking this minute in one of the sailors' inns along the docks. My da was long gone afore I were born."

"Could your mother not tell you about him?" I asked.

Again the harsh laugh. "I don't know if my

ma knew who he was. Even if she did, she were confused in the head when I were old enough to remember. She died when I were just a nipper."

"I'm sorry," I said.

"I ain't looking for pity. I'm just saying. Besides, I had a big family."

I frowned, wondering where all this was going.

"You're a real innocent, Georgie," Davy went on, his tone much lighter. "I grew up in a workhouse for the poor. When me ma went strange in the head and after she died, the women in the workhouse looked after me. You could say I had twenty mothers."

His face took on a wistful expression. "Best days of my life, I reckon. Always someone nearby to fuss over me, and other boys my age to play with. The women came and went, but I loved them all.

"Point is, Georgie boy, I been looking after myself as long as I can remember. I seen ups and downs. There've been wonderful times and times I'd rather not dwell upon, but I'm still here, ain't I?"

I nodded, although Davy wasn't looking for an answer. "You been lucky," he went on. "A ma and da to care for you, put a dinner on the table and see to new boots and jacket when the old ones wear out. I don't begrudge your luck. Fact is, I envy it;

but life ain't like that. Unless you'll be happy sitting at a clerk's desk the rest of your days, you got to go out and seek your own adventures. Now, if I read you right, Georgie, I reckon you want adventure, so time's come to make a choice. Go home to your nice warm bed and your clerk's desk, or come with me tonight for a taste of the other side of life."

I thought for a long time as Davy watched me in the moonlight, but I didn't think there was ever any doubt about my answer. "I'll come with you," I said.

"That's the spirit," Davy said, jumping off the bollard and slapping me on the back. "Now, we'd best hurry if we're to meet my friend."

It was the first I'd heard of a friend, but I didn't have time to ask. Davy was off through the streets of Woolwich and I had to almost run to keep up. To my shock, we headed back up Church Hill toward my house. I kept to the shadows as much as possible, even though the chances of anyone who might recognize me being up and about at this hour were slim. We passed number 58, swung round the corner and farther up the hill to the square shape of St. Mary Magdalene Church. A figure stepped out of the shadows by the cemetery gate. "Where you bin?" a gruff voice asked, "And oo's this?"

"I'm here, ain't I, Jim?" Davy replied. "And my

friend Georgie's here to help with the heavy work."

"Don't look much good," Jim said dismissively. "Long streak o' misery." He was a short man, but powerfully built, and his face was covered in pox scars. He leered at me, showing the dark gaps where he was missing teeth.

"He ain't getting a cut," Davy said. "I'll share my part. Let's get on, it's near as bright as day."

Jim grunted but turned back to the shadows, where I noticed a small handcart sitting in the trees. He took out two wooden shovels and tossed one each to Davy and me. I examined mine closely, surprised to see a shovel made from wood instead of iron.

"Makes less noise when you're digging," Davy explained.

Jim lifted out a heavy iron bar and a coil of rope, and led the way round to the back of the church.

"What are we doing here?" I whispered.

"Digging for treasure," Davy replied with a laugh.

A graveyard would be a good place to hide treasure, I thought, but it was certainly eerie. The tilted gravestones and statues of angels stood out a ghostly white in the moonlight. As we moved between them, I had the feeling that I saw movement out of the corner of my eye, but when I turned my head they stood as cold and still as the people whose graves they marked.

My brother, Thomas, was buried over by the far wall, but I deliberately avoided looking in that direction. I preferred to remember the day of his funeral — a busy occasion in comforting daylight — and the times Mother and I had come to place flowers by his simple headstone.

I wondered if what we were about to dig up were the proceeds from some robbery. What was I getting into? I thought of dropping the shovel and running, but fear of Jim made me hesitate. Then it was too late.

"Here," Jim said, stopping in front of a mound of fresh dark earth. A large bouquet of flowers lay at one end. The moonlight was bright enough to read the writing on the attached card: *To our beloved son, Simon.*

"Nice new un," Jim said, kicking the flowers aside. He scanned the surrounding shadows. "We'd best be quick, now. Dig where them pretty flowers were."

Davy thrust his shovel into the soft earth. This must be where the treasure was hidden, but what was it and why was it here?

"Stop gawking and dig!" Jim ordered. "'Less you want the daylight to catch you."

Reluctantly, I joined Davy and began work. It was easy going through the freshly turned damp earth and we were soon both standing in the hole we had created. I was concentrating on our work, trying not to think what we were doing, so it came as a surprise when my shovel thumped against wood. With a shudder, I realized I was standing on a rough coffin. Davy scraped earth off the lid.

"Break it open," Jim ordered, handing Davy the iron bar and dropping the rope down beside him. Throwing the shovel aside, Davy began prying the coffin lid up. The cheap wood splintered easily. I stepped back from the dark hole Davy was creating.

"The treasure's *in* the coffin?" I exclaimed, clambering out of the grave.

"'Course it is," Jim said. "Where'd you think? Now get down there and 'elp Davy."

"No," I said. I surprised myself with the firmness of my denial, but there was no way I was going back into that fresh grave.

Jim's hand grabbed me by my jacket collar and hauled me round until our faces were mere inches apart. His breath stank of stale alcohol. "You get down there and 'elp Davy get that body up or it'll be *you* in the cart sold for a few shillings."

Suddenly I realized the full horror of what we

were doing. "You're a Resurrection Man," I said, my voice barely above a whisper. "You're going to sell this body to a hospital to be cut up for the students to learn."

Jim turned his head to the side. "God love us, Davy," he said. "Where'd you find this idiot?"

I thought I saw my chance and lashed out at Jim, catching him a solid blow to the side of his head, but he barely flinched and his grip only tightened. His head flashed forward and caught me a dizzying blow to the forehead. I slumped to the ground in a daze.

From what sounded like a great distance, I heard Jim's voice. "Never mind that un, Davy. Your friend 'ere'll make more. They don't come fresher than 'im."

Through the haze of pain, I struggled to make sense of what was going on. Things seemed to be happening very slowly. Jim was a dark figure crouching beside me. Something in his hand glinted in the moonlight. "We'll bleed 'im 'ere, throw 'im in the cart and take 'im down to the 'ospital. Easy money."

"Wait up, Jim. I've got a better idea."

Why was Davy's voice so unconcerned?

"What?" Jim grunted.

Out of the corner of my eye, I saw Davy scramble

out of the grave. He came over and draped an arm around Jim's shoulder. "We do him," Davy said calmly, "and that's murder, straight up. The Peelers catch us and it's a rope around our necks outside Newgate Prison, for certain. Let's just take the fresh one out of the grave and be done."

"And leave this un to blab what we done to the world?"

"He won't say nothing. Will you, Georgie boy?"

"No," I mumbled. Strangely, I felt no fear. It was as if I were watching a play that didn't involve me.

"Ain't taking that chance," Jim said. "'Course, you could always join 'im in the cart."

"Now, now, Jim." Davy's voice was smooth and soothing as he leaned in closer. "We don't want to do anything hasty, do we?"

There was a sudden movement and Jim gasped as Davy pushed hard against his chest. Jim waved his arms about in slow motion. His mouth opened and closed like a fish stranded on the beach, and something dark ran down his chin. He gave a surprisingly soft, gurgling cough, as Davy shoved him into the open grave.

"You all right, Georgie boy?" Davy asked. He wiped a long, narrow knife on Jim's jacket.

"You *killed* him," I said slowly, still dazed stupid by the blow to my head.

"Well, he were going to kill *you*," Davy pointed out. "Would you rather that happened?"

"No," I said. Things slowly came back into focus and time began moving at its normal speed. It registered even more fully that my new friend had just killed someone.

"I reckon we'd best get you home, Georgie. Afore you get into more trouble." Davy looked back at the open grave. "Shame about the body, but it's too late now." He helped me to my feet and we stumbled back out onto the road.

"You were going to sell that man's body," I said as I struggled to make sense of all that had happened. "You're a body snatcher."

"I was just there to help retrieve it," Davy explained as we walked back down Church Hill. "Jim were the one with contacts. He's been a Resurrection Man for many a year. One of the best, they do say, but business ain't too good these days. Used to be only gallows bodies were allowed for dissection — big demand for fresh bodies then — but now anyone can be cut up. Jim couldn't change. Body snatching were all he knew. He could only sell to some very suspect characters what wanted corpses for God knows what purpose. Prices dropped way down. Poor Jim started drinking hard to drown his sorrows. See where it got him."

I stopped walking as we neared my house. My head ached, my mouth was dry with fear and my legs were barely able to support me. It was as if I were trapped in a nightmare. "If this is your idea of adventure," I said, turning to face Davy, "I want none of it. Maybe I'll stay a clerk, or maybe I'll find another path, but it will not be yours. I do not wish ever to see you again."

"Well, there's gratitude," Davy said. He seemed unconcerned by what I'd said. "I saved your life not a half hour ago."

"And I thank you for that from the bottom of my heart, but it was *you* who put my life in danger a half hour before that. I envied you your freedom and adventures, but now I see the other side of it, and I want nothing more to do with it — or you." I was desperate to break into a run, to get as far from Davy as I could, and quickly, but I forced myself to walk casually down the hill to our house. At the door I stopped and brushed off as much of the damp earth as possible. Then I slipped inside. The last thing I heard before I closed the door was Davy whistling a jaunty tune as he strolled past on the street.

Chapter 3
An Adventure Born
Woolwich, England, 1845

It took me many weeks to put the horrors of the graveyard behind me. In that time, I saw no more of Davy and assumed that that episode of my life was behind me. I continued working at my dull desk, until one day I saw in the newspaper that Sir John Franklin was about to lead a wonderful expedition to the Arctic to complete the Northwest Passage. That evening I ran all the way home, determined to persuade Father to contact Sir John and call in the favour that the great man had promised at Trafalgar. I would go north with Sir John and begin a new life of adventure.

Father hesitated, but I persuaded him that this was my great chance. Mother was harder to convince. She saw Thomas go to sea and come home in a coffin and did not want that to happen again, but the weight of Father's and my arguments eventually swayed her.

"There's no safer way for the boy to have an adventure than to go north with Sir John on this expedition," Father explained. "The ships are the strongest and best Her Majesty's Navy can supply. Word is that they will be provisioned with all essentials for three years — "

"Three years!" Mother exclaimed. "George will be gone *three* years in that land of ice and snow?"

"No. No, dear," Father said, trying another tack. "The expedition will take but a season, two at most. The extra is merely a precaution. Ice is a fickle thing, and who knows what wonders they may find to detain them."

"Even so, to be up there, in such cold."

"The ships have a system of pipes that bring heat to all parts of the living quarters," Father explained. "I've read about it in the newspapers. Young George shall be as snug as a bug in a rug."

"And there are to be *real* steam engines," I added.

"Indeed there are," Father said. "Each vessel shall have a complete steam engine from the Greenwich railway, and the coal to run them. Even should the winds and currents be contrary once the ships reach the narrow channels of those Arctic lands, they need only fire up the engines and be on their way as easily as if they were sailing down the Thames River itself. No expense is to be spared and Sir John is to have the best of everything. Every new-fangled invention that our imagination can conceive will be represented, from portable, inflatable boats to image-fixing devices."

"Imagine that, Mother! *Pictures* of all that we shall discover and learn. When we return, there will be the most amazing exhibition of illustrations and discoveries, perhaps set against a painted diorama of the northern lands. People will flock from all around the world to marvel at what we have accomplished."

Father laughed. "Do not worry in the least. Our boy will be as safe and comfortable as if he were asleep in his bed upstairs. All the talk of the formidable Northwest Passage is simply put about to sell newspapers. Thanks to the exploits of Parry and Ross — on expeditions in which not a single man was lost, I might add — the unknown part of the Passage is little more than the distance of a coach ride from where we sit now down to Dover."

"Then why go at all?" Mother asked, not quite ready to be convinced.

"To learn," Father replied. "The route is known, but there is still so much we do not know about the exotic realms of our Earth. Sir John leads a scientific venture. Its primary purpose is to study everything from the smallest swimming creature in the ocean to the largest whalefish, from the strange magnetic fluctuations near the Pole to the speech of the peoples who live thereabouts. The expedition would establish the Arctic and all the treasures it contains as part of our growing empire. What an honour it would be to have George a part of that."

Mother's worries could not remain firm in the face of Father's persuasion and my enthusiasm. Eventually she surrendered and gave me her blessing. William and Alexander, who had listened to all our talk from the corner where they were playing with their red-coated lead soldiers, gave three rousing cheers.

The very next day Father wrote to Sir John, and in a matter of days received a reply. It stated that I was to be a lowly cabin boy on HMS *Erebus* and was required to report for duty on April 28, 1845, at the Woolwich dock. My mother busied herself, frantically knitting endless socks, scarves and gloves to shield me from the cold, while I devoured every book I could find on the northern lands.

It seemed an age until April 28, but I filled much of my time gazing at Sir John's ships, *Erebus* and *Terror*, being prepared for the voyage. I sat above the dry docks at Woolwich, watching as the heavy iron plates were added to protect the hulls from the ice, and as entire steam locomotives were lowered into the ships' holds. The ships swarmed with workmen rigging, painting and hammering. An endless stream of uniformed officers and dignitaries came to inspect the progress.

Eventually the great day drew near and the ships were given a coat of paint, white for the three masts, black for the hull and a broad yellow stripe around. On the morning *Erebus* was to be floated, Father and I arrived at the dock early. We watched as the dry dock was flooded and the vessel, my home for the next year or two, floated out onto the river. She sat low in the water as she went through her paces but, to my unpracticed eye, she appeared stable and safe.

In the afternoon, *Erebus* approached her moorings. Many of the crew were already aboard and the open deck was crowded. Those not engaged in docking leaned on the rail and stared at the small crowd that had gathered to watch the display. I remember noticing a young officer who directed the crew with cheerful shouts. I was so excited that I barely heard Father explain the vessel's benefits.

"She will see you through the Passage," Father said. "After all, with James Ross, she and *Terror* took the worst that three years of the Antarctic oceans could throw at her, and she has been even further strengthened for your voyage." He laughed and clapped me on the back. "I doubt the ice you encounter will present a serious problem."

As *Erebus* bumped gently against the dock and sailors ran to secure the lines, I scanned the men leaning on the ship's rail. They were a rough-looking crew and I felt a sudden nervousness at being in their company. Then I froze. One of the figures was waving at me.

"Someone you know?" my father asked.

The figure was smiling, but I couldn't forget the last time I had seen him, plunging his knife into Jim's chest. "It's . . . He's . . . " I stammered, "someone I met down by the river."

Father didn't seem to notice my discomfort. "Then you will have a companion on board."

I didn't answer. I was too confused. What was Davy doing on the *Erebus*? How would I be able to avoid him on such a small vessel? He seemed quite jolly, waving hard and smiling broadly. Weakly, I returned his wave.

I waited, fidgeted and tried not to meet Davy's eye as *Erebus* was securely docked and a gangway run alongside. Then the young officer I had seen on deck came ashore, laughing and joking with a companion.

"I don't see Sir John," Father said, looking

around. "Surely he would have disembarked first if he was aboard." He pushed me forward. "Go and introduce yourself to the officer, George. Be polite."

I edged forward and stood by the officer. Up close he was older than I had thought, but his chubby features made him look young. He was hatless and had curly ginger hair. His eyes sparkled and a smile continually played around his mouth. At length he noticed me. I removed my cap. "I am George Chambers," I said. "I was told to report to Sir John Franklin as a cabin boy."

"Ah, Chambers," the officer said, his smile broadening. "Sir John said you would be joining us. He is staying up in town for the time being — won't live on board until we are ready to sail. The advantage of being famous, I suppose.

"I am Commander James Fitzjames. Your duties will be split between Sir John and myself. Do you live nearby?"

"Just up on Church Hill, sir."

"Excellent. Head home and get your kit in order. *Terror* will perform her trials tomorrow. Time enough then to come aboard and begin learning the ropes. I'm sure your mother won't object to one last night at home."

"She won't, sir. Thank you."

Fitzjames nodded and turned back to his companion.

As I headed away with my father, I scanned the ship's rail, but there was no sign of Davy.

The following day I boarded *Erebus*, feeling very nautical hauling the chest full of my kit up the gangway, and reported to Mr. Fitzjames. He welcomed me and passed me on to the purser, Mr. Osmer, a jovial fellow who showed me where to sling my hammock in the crew mess deck and where to stow my chest — which also served as a seat for meals. Then he ran through my duties.

"You are first and foremost a servant, boy," he told me, "and your primary duties are to Sir John and Mr. Fitzjames. You will help the stewards serve them, and whichever other officers dine with Sir John, every evening. You will fetch whatever they require, carry messages for them, wash their clothes and keep their quarters clean."

I nodded. These were things I had guessed as my duties. However, Osmer wasn't finished. "A cabin boy is the lowest being on board ship. When not attending to the officers' needs, you will be at the beck and call of any and all who might require your services. You will help the cook prepare meals in the galley and carry food to the crew before you eat. You will learn all the workings of the ship, from swabbing the deck to the uses of every line and rope on board. By the time we return home, you will be more comfortable scrambling up the rigging than you will be on dry land. You will learn to trim the sails, stand watch in all weathers and work the helm."

I must have looked overwhelmed, because Osmer slapped me on the back and said, "Don't you worry, lad. You'll learn in time and it will give your days variety. Besides, there's one thing you won't have to do on this voyage."

"What's that?" I asked, glad there was one task I would escape.

"We're not going to war, so you will not have the duties of powder monkey in battle. It is good to know all aspects of the workings of a ship. The knowledge will be a great help should you decide to undertake a life in the Navy."

"A life as a cabin boy?" I asked.

"To begin, yes, but many a cabin boy who has applied himself has risen far above that station. Francis Drake himself began his seafaring life as a boy, and there's many an admiral who can trace his career back to being a lowly officer's servant. And" — Osmer leaned closer and lowered his voice — "in my opinion, you'll find no better officers to serve than either Sir John or Mr. Fitzjames. Now, there's work to be done loading the stores."

Chapter 4
Old and New Friends
Aboard *Erebus*, 1845

I was shocked to discover that Osmer had set me to work beside Davy. I was nervous that my angry parting from him would sour our relationship and be a problem on the long voyage. However, Davy didn't seem concerned, and even smiled and nodded to me as we began our duties.

We worked all day, dragging and lifting crates and sacks and rolling barrels down into the hold, and were so busy that we barely had time to exchange a word. All the while, Osmer, with proud precision, listed our supplies: 8 tons biscuit; 31 tons flour; 15 tons salt beef and pork; 5 tons sugar; thousands of pounds each of tea, soap and candles; and 2 tons chocolate. We even had 2000 gallons of concentrated spirits, 100 gallons of wine for the sick, 500 gallons of lemon juice and 100 pounds of pepper. There were also many thousands of pounds of preserved meat, soup and vegetables in cans, not to mention the luxuries brought on board by the officers.

That afternoon Davy and I were carrying jars of lemon juice aboard when Davy slipped and dropped his load. The jar didn't break, but Davy cursed loudly, attracting Osmer's attention.

"You might well cuss, boy," Osmer remarked. "What's in them jars'll save your life."

"Save my life?" Davy scoffed as he lifted the heavy jar back onto his shoulder. "The rum we carry might do that, but the juice of lemons?"

Osmer let out a short laugh. "You're no deep-sea sailor, lad, that's for certain. You've never seen a grown man whimper in agony; unable to move for the red-hot pain in his joints; his lips black; his mouth bleeding; and his teeth falling out as every scar he's ever collected oozes blood like it were a new cut."

Davy stopped adjusting his load and we both stared at Osmer.

"Scurvy, lads — sailor's curse on a long voyage such as ours. There's summat we need that ain't in salt pork nor chocolate. Summat that's in lemon juice. So you boys drink your ounce of juice when Mr. Fitzjames calls you up on deck every day. Else the scurvy'll get you for certain. Now get on with your work."

Osmer turned away. I vowed to take my lemon juice every day. I turned to see if Osmer's words had had a similar effect on Davy. "Old fool," was all he said.

It was near the bell for the evening meal by the time Osmer released us from our duties. All I wanted was to find a corner and rest my aching body, but Davy wanted to talk. "So we meet again, Master Chambers," he began.

I grunted an acknowledgement. I wanted time to sort out my confused emotions. It had been a long time since I had last seen Davy in the grave-yard, and if I was honest, a part of me was pleased to see his smiling face at *Erebus*'s rail. But he was involved in body snatching and I had seen him kill a man — even if it was a man who was trying to kill me. It was all so complicated.

"Look, Georgie," Davy said when I didn't respond. "I ain't a saint — never pretended that I were — and I done some things that I ain't proud of. But life ain't easy. Now, I reckon we got on well enough afore we met Jim, so we got two choices. We're stuck here on the same few square yards of deck for God knows how long. We can each pretend the other don't exist, or we can get on as best we can. After this adventure, we can go our own ways and never say hello to each other again, but for now, let's pretend Jim and the graveyard never happened."

Davy grinned at me and held out his hand. I hesitated, but he was right. We either got on or condemned ourselves to months of misery. I took his hand.

Davy hauled me towards him and slapped me on the back. "So now that we're friends again," he said as we drew apart, "what role do you play in this great undertaking?"

"I am cabin boy to Sir John and Mr. Fitzjames," I replied.

"Same as me," Davy said, "but I got Lieutenants Gore, Le Vesconte and Fairholme to attend to."

Before I could think of anything to say, the bell for the evening meal rang. "Come on, Georgie," Davy said, "that's the call for you and me. We got to work for our supper afore we attend to the high and mighty."

We climbed down to the mess deck and headed over to the large, black stove where the cook, Richard Wall stood, ladling stew into buckets for distribution to the crew. Down each side of the deck, tables hung suspended from the deck above, and the crew sat on their chests. Each table of eight men received a bucket of stew and a wooden board stacked with biscuits and mugs of tea.

Following Davy's lead, I lifted a bucket and board and set off, wondering how I would manage this when the ship was rolling at sea. The first table I came to was occupied by seven Royal Marines. They were older than the average sailor and looked hard. Most were in shirt sleeves, but two wore their distinctive red coats, unbuttoned. Several sported tattoos, mostly crowns and anchors or a nautical scene. I placed the board and bucket beside them, but couldn't help but stare at the silver epaulettes with the anchor in the middle. Father had shown me his epaulettes and I wondered if this was how he had looked in his days as a marine.

"What you looking at, boy?" one of the men wearing a red coat asked. He was skinny, with a long face and prominent cheekbones. His hair was dark and curled over his ears, although it was thinning on top. He had a short, ugly scar on his forehead and wore a bright red kerchief knotted around his neck.

"N–nothing," I stammered. "It's just . . . My father was a marine."

"What ship?" the man demanded.

"He was on the *Bellerophon* at Trafalgar," I said proudly.

Everyone at the table turned to look at me. "The old *Billy Ruffian*," the man said. "Now *that* were a fine old ship." The others at the table nodded in agreement. The marine stood up and smiled, exposing a mouthful of tobacco-stained teeth, several of which showed signs of rot. He was tall — over 6 foot, I guessed — and he unfolded his long, thin limbs like a spider uncurling. He held out his hand. "I'm pleased to meet the son of a marine from the *Billy Ruffian*," he said. "My name's William Braine."

"I'm George Chambers," I replied. We shook hands.

"You know that Sir John himself was on board for that fight?" Braine said as he sat back down.

"I know," I blurted out. "My father saved his life."

"Did he indeed? Well, young George Chambers, I look forward to having a chance to hear that story."

"Are we going to have to wait all night for our dinner while you natter with your new friends?" a sailor from another table shouted at me. I grabbed another bucket and board and continued with my duties.

Once every table was served, Davy and I took stew, biscuits and tea to ours. The stew was not too bad. It contained carrots, turnips, onions and occasional chunks of meat that a grizzled old sailor said was horse.

"You'll be glad of a nice piece of horse where

we're going," he said, a smile creasing his weather-beaten face.

"What do you mean?" I asked. "Are there horses in the Arctic?"

The man snorted. "This here young pup thinks there's *horses* up where we're going." Several men at the table sniggered.

"I don't," I said, blushing with embarrassment at my stupid comment. "But we have enough good food with us to eat well for three years or more. Why should we wish for horsemeat?"

For a long moment, the man soaked a biscuit in his stew. Then he sucked at it with relish and looked at me. "I worked the whalers," he said eventually. "All around Baffin's Bay and Davis Strait. We had food, too — not as good as this, mind you, but good enough. We always set out thinking everything'd be fine and this'd be the season we made our fortune in whale oil. But them northern waters got a way of their own." Everyone at the table was listening intently.

"That ice's like a living thing, trying to trick you, draw you in, trap you. I've seen ships frozen in with the crew still in them, stone dead. Frozen as hard as rock. Once saw a captain froze at his desk, quill still in his hand. We had to break both his legs to get him out the cabin door." The man looked round us all, his mouth open in a broken-toothed grin.

"Pay no mind to old Bill," Davy said, breaking the long silence. "If you believe everything he says, I've a magic brass lamp to sell you."

Nervous laughter ran round the table, but Bill went on. "You believe what you wish, lad, it's no matter to me. But I'll tell you this. I were a cabin boy once, back in '27 on the good ship *Anne* out of Whitby. We was nipped in the ice off Greenland — never was a place more wrongly named. We just made it ashore over the ice. It were three weeks afore leads opened and another whaler could reach us. Those weeks would've killed us for sure if the local natives hadn't brought us seal meat to eat."

He paused a moment for effect and then continued. "Or else the others would've killed and eaten the cabin boy."

The shocked silence that followed this pronouncement was broken by Bill's wheezing laugh. He took a long clay pipe out of his jacket and proceeded to light it, sending clouds of harsh tobacco smoke into the air.

"If it's so bad up north," I said. "Why did you sign up for this voyage?"

"Simple," Bill replied. "We get double pay. And

in advance. 'Fore we sail, I'll have twenty-three pounds in my pocket. That's plenty for a good drink and to keep the wife and nippers in food for a year or more."

Other heads nodded in agreement. I realized that for all the fine words in the newspapers about the glory of Empire, Discovery and Science, most of the men were simply on board for the extra pay.

A bell rang and a flurry of activity broke out — men stowed chests, hauled tables up and cleared away buckets and plates. Davy and I were busy scrubbing Wall's pots and pans. "Do you think those stories are true?" I asked.

"Maybe, some bits," Davy said with a shrug. "Old sailors do love to tell tales, 'specially if they've a landsman to impress. Mind you, even if they are true, there's a world of difference 'tween a worm-eaten whaler with a greedy captain chancing his luck in Davis Strait, and the expedition we're on. Besides, I've seen worse than his stories in Field Lane and Saffron Hill."

That night after I struggled into my hammock and lay listening to the other forty or so men snoring and quietly grumbling in our confined, dark space, I wondered about Bill's tales. Certainly Davy was right and our situation was radically different from those of whalers, but the talk of starvation, freezing death and the possibility of cannibalism unsettled me as I drifted off to sleep.

Chapter 5
Learning the Ropes
The North Atlantic, 1845

My aching muscles were becoming used to the hard work on board ship by the time we were towed down to Greenhithe for final preparations. *Erebus* and *Terror* fitted snugly into a small dock beside an inn where Sir John and Lady Franklin took a room on the upper floor. From her window, she could watch the activity on the ships and hear the rumble of the supplies being hauled along the cobbled lane beside the inn. Sir John spent an increasing amount of time with us and impressed everyone with his good humour, generosity and fairness.

One day, Mr. Beard arrived with the Daguerrotype image-fixing apparatus that we were to take north to record our exploits. As a first record and as a way of training Second Master Henry Collins in the use of the apparatus, images were made of all the officers of *Erebus* and Captain Crozier of *Terror*. It was a cold, miserable day — Lieutenant Fairholme was obliged to borrow Mr. Fitzjames's jacket — and Sir John was suffering much from the effects of influenza. Each officer sat most seriously for the images, except Mr. Fitzjames, who picked up his telescope and smiled at Mr. Beard when the second image was taken.

The Saturday before we sailed, the four thousand cans of Mr. Goldner's meat, soup and vegetables finally arrived. As we struggled to load them on board, Mr. Osmer grumbled incessantly. "Penny-pinching fools," he said as we sweated. "The Navy Board picks the lowest bid for supply and we only get our food at the last minute."

"At least it's all here," I said.

"Aye," Osmer agreed, "but done in such a rush that I'll warrant we find a goodly number of cans blown and rotten when we come to open them, and I doubt if Mr. Goldner has an office in Greenland where we can complain."

On the Sunday, Sir John conducted Divine Service for the assembled crews. He spoke eloquently on our duties and the importance of the task upon which we were embarking. After the service, a dove, which everyone except the miserable sailor Bill considered a good omen, alighted on the masthead. The day was filled with hope and much speculation on our great adventure.

Never in my life had I been so excited as I

was when we cast off at ten-thirty that Monday morning, the nineteenth of May, 1845. The *Erebus* led our small flotilla out onto the river. She was followed by *Terror*, our supply ship *Barretto Junior* and two tugs, *Rattler* and *Blazer*. Laden as we were, our sails filled with the morning breeze and we presented a splendid sight, flags of every description snapping in the wind and every officer dressed in formal finery.

The embankment was thronged with well-wishers, many waving brightly-coloured cloths and cheering lustily. The cheering was echoed by ourselves and by the lowing of the ten live oxen being carried aboard *Barretto Junior*. The river itself was rich with boats of all description, many bedecked in fluttering bunting. Horns provided a deafening background music, and every vessel, from the smallest rowboat to the greatest warship, offered us three cheers as we passed by on the tide.

On that proud day, the future seemed endless and anything possible.

The voyage up the coast of Britain was a continual struggle against storms and contrary winds, however. Several crew, Davy among them, were sick from the violent motion of the ships, but I was pleasantly surprised at how well my stomach stood up to the ordeal. I had little appetite at first, but what I did eat stayed where it should.

"Kill me now," Davy muttered. I had come on deck to escape the foul stink of sickness below and found him huddled by the rail, arms wrapped around his knees. "A quick death would be a mercy."

The ship lurched violently as it slid down a huge wave. I grabbed a rigging line and Davy groaned. I often came up in the rough weather to inhale some fresh air and watch the angry sea.

I was often accompanied by the ship's dog, Neptune, a large, hairy beast, of the type called after Newfoundland. He had a stronger stomach than many of the sailors, and the gentlest disposition I had ever found in an animal. For a scratch behind the ear, he was prepared to follow me anywhere on board.

"You'll feel better soon," I said to reassure Davy.

"I won't survive to feel better," he said. He was as pale as the ship's canvas and losing weight from not being able to hold food in his stomach. "Next time I retch I'll bring up my heart and lungs. There's nothing else down there."

There was no comforting Davy when he was suffering these bouts of seasickness. Neptune and I left him in peace. By the time we finally docked at Stromness in the Orkney Islands, he was feeling better and there were signs of his sense of humour returning.

At Stromness we replenished our fresh-water supply from the well there and bade farewell to *Rattler* and *Blazer*. I was surprised on going ashore that I had become so used to the rolling and plunging of the ship's deck that I had trouble walking on solid ground. Davy stayed on board to recover.

In contrast, the voyage across the Atlantic was calm. That is not to say it was boring. Davy and I were kept busy with a multitude of new tasks. One day we were given over to the care of Robert Sinclair, Captain of the Foretop.

"Ye cannot live aboard one o' Her Majesty's vessels wi'out learnin' to climb the ropes," he told us in his broad Scots accent. Sinclair was only twenty-five years old, but had been at sea since the age of twelve and had developed immensely strong arms from a life clambering up the rigging and crawling along the yards. Even though it was the calmest day we had yet seen, with only a steady following wind, I was nervous at the prospect of climbing high above the deck with only ropes to hold me there.

"Best way's just to do it," Sinclair said. "You

first." He pointed at me. "Climb that riggin' on the foremast."

I swallowed hard and headed for the rail, which I had to climb over to get onto the complex of ropes that would be my ladder up the mast. I had a moment's hesitation as I swung out over the dark, rushing water of the Atlantic; then I was climbing. Before I knew it, I was enjoying myself. The wind whistled through the rigging around me, the heavy canvas sail snapped and the spars and mast creaked. It was almost like flying and I was soon at the main spar.

"Step out onto that rope below the spar," Sinclair shouted through cupped hands. "See how ye can lean over the spar and grasp those other ropes that'll furl the sail."

The step from the rigging to the spar rope required taking one hand off the rigging and stretching over the yawning gulf down to the deck to place a foot on a single swinging rope. I took a deep breath and stepped.

To my immense relief I felt the rope under my foot and the solid spar against my chest. I brought my other foot over and grasped the spar for all I was worth, reaching over it to hold the ropes that hung down on the other side. I had seen sailors lined along the spar rope to furl or unfurl the sails on Mr. Fitzjames's commands.

Joy surged through me. I was confident and secure and, for the first time since I had stepped up the gangway at Woolwich, I felt like a true sailor.

As if in celebration of my achievement, the sleek, silvery backs of a school of dolphins broke the surface on either side of *Erebus*'s bow. They gambolled in some complicated game, crossing and recrossing our bow many times before they shot off to starboard in pursuit of some other entertainment.

"Good work, lad," Sinclair shouted. "Now you," he said to Davy. "Come along now."

I looked down to see Davy hesitating with one foot on the rail. "Come on, Davy," I yelled. "It's magical up here."

Gingerly, he stepped onto the rigging and began a slow climb. He stopped a lot and eventually Sinclair shouted, "Hurry along, lad. Ye can't be a sailor if ye can't climb the riggin'."

"I'd rather be a Resurrection Man," Davy said under his breath as he reached the spar. He was breathing hard. Beads of sweat stood out on his face.

I moved along the spar to make room for him. "Come out onto the spar."

Davy glanced down and a look of horror swept over his face. "I can't."

"It's all right," I said as reassuringly as possible. "Put your left foot onto the rope I'm standing on and throw your arm over the spar. One step and you're here."

Davy looked uncertain, but he tentatively lifted his foot off the rigging. At that moment a gust of wind snapped the sail with a loud crack and the spar rope swung wildly. Davy lurched back and clung desperately onto the rigging, his knuckles white and his breath coming in gasps. I tried to persuade him to try again, and Sinclair threatened him with flogging, but neither of us could get Davy to move. Eventually I climbed back onto the rigging and helped Davy down to the deck.

Sinclair thumped me hard on the back. "Well done," he said.

Then, turning to Davy, he added, "You'll need to keep trying," before striding away.

I tried to comfort Davy, but he simply stalked off and kept to himself for the rest of the day. I had planned to talk to him before we slung our hammocks that night, but he was tight in with old Bill, and playing some gambling game.

The thrill of my achievement on the rigging

stayed with me, but there was another feeling lurking beneath the pride. I wasn't happy that I felt this way . . . but I *was* glad that I had found something I could do better than Davy.

Chapter 6
Into the Northwest Passage
Beechey Island, 1845

On July 14 we caught our first sight of the Greenland coast through the swirling fog. It was not at
all like its name, but a rugged place of black rock
cut by white furrows and ravines of snow with
huge rivers of blue ice cascading off the moun-
tains into the ocean. It was a desolate place, and
for the first time I understood the power of the
land we were about to enter.

The ice rivers had dropped large bergs that were
scattered over the calm dark-blue sea. We passed
close to one fantastically formed berg and many
of the crew lined the rail in silence to wonder at
this immense gleaming cathedral of ice, spark-
ling in the midnight sun. Despite its size, it did
not look out of place in this vast land, yet had it
been placed at Woolwich, it would have blocked
the entire river.

Icebergs became commonplace, but every day
we sailed north presented those of us new to these
lands with another wonder. We had nights so

clear it seemed I could reach up from the deck and pluck the incredibly bright stars. I spotted whales of all descriptions gambolling about our bow. Perhaps strangest of all was ice-blink, the reflection of the sun off distant ice that Mr. Fitzjames said looked like nothing so much as a small town on fire about 20 miles off.

Mr. Goodsir was Assistant Surgeon to Mr. Stanley, but he was also our naturalist. In that role he spent many hours leaning over the rail with a drift net, catching all manner of strange creatures that he poked, prodded, drew and finally put away in bottles of foul-smelling preservative.

Eventually we reached Disko, where we transferred the last of our supplies from the *Barretto Junior*. Mr. Fitzjames tested the magnetic equipment and even attempted to paddle around the bay in one of the Esquimaux boats, called kayaks. Then we said goodbye to civilization and set off to cross Baffin Bay.

At the end of July, while awaiting a favourable wind, we anchored to a massive iceberg. Despite our growing familiarity with these objects, I was fearful that the berg might suddenly topple over and crush us. I mentioned my fear to Davy, but he merely scoffed. I was tempted to bring up his terror on the rigging, but thought better of it. He was already beginning to spend much of his free time with Bill and his cronies, and I did not wish to drive a wedge between us. As it turned out, my fears were groundless, as the berg proved as solid as the Isle of Wight.

As August came, we exchanged greetings with a couple of whaling ships before the wind turned favourable and we headed west into Lancaster Sound and the true beginning of our adventure.

One day in mid-August, we passed a sheltered bay at Beechey Island. "That would make a good winter harbour," Mr. Fitzjames said to me after he had finished explaining more duties involved in standing a watch.

"Is it not too early in the year to think of wintering?" I ventured.

"Indeed, we should still have several weeks of good sailing time left before winter sets in. However, we have a Term Date to meet at some secure place where we can build a magnetic camp and take some precise readings."

"Term Date?" I asked.

"August 29," Mr. Fitzjames explained. "On that day, throughout the British Empire — which as you know means around the world — readings of the Earth's magnetic field will be taken. Ours will be the most important of those readings, since we are at the most northerly point on the globe. If all goes well, our work will greatly contribute to our imperfect understanding of the strange magnetic currents that run through our planet and by which we find our way with the compass."

"But we have two weeks until the twenty-ninth," I said.

"True enough, but Parry found few safe anchorages until he reached Winter Harbour many miles to the west. Should we not be able to progress that far, we must return here by the Term Date. After that, we will have little time left for progress and, I believe, will do better to encamp here and use the remaining good weather to send out small exploring parties to scout the land and our possible routes for next season."

Things turned out almost as Mr. Fitzjames had foretold. Our way west was blocked by a terrifying river of ice and we retreated to Beechey Island and set up a magnetic camp on nearby Cape Riley.

Through September and October we occupied ourselves in hunting, exploring as far afield as possible, establishing shore camps and preparing the ships for the coming cold. As soon as the sea froze, we marked out paths across the ice with tall posts so we could travel between the ships and the shore, even in a blizzard.

As the days shortened and the ice locked us in, work managing the ship decreased and Davy's and my duties narrowed to our responsibilities to Sir John and Mr. Fitzjames and the other officers.

One day early in November I was serving Mr. Fitzjames soup in his cabin as he warmed up following his return from the Cape Riley magnetic camp.

"Well, young George," he said, "we shall not complete the Passage in one year, as some had thought."

"Aye, sir," I agreed, "but I think we have found a good, sheltered place to spend the winter, and we shall learn much about this land."

"That's the spirit, boy," Mr. Fitzjames said with a laugh. "We are here to learn, and the exploring parties have discovered much already. We shall have quite the collection of knowledge to take back home, not least the disgusting things Mr. Goodsir seems intent on keeping in bottles everywhere."

Mr. Fitzjames took a spoonful of soup and furrowed his brow. "But we must also send out more hunting parties before hard winter sets in," he said. "The canned food is a disappointment."

"I heard some was spoiled," I said. "Is it much?"

"Too much. I fear Mr. Goldner overreached himself in filling our order. There are signs of shoddy workmanship and spoiled food. The soup" — he waved his spoon over the bowl in front of him — "and the vegetables do not seem so bad, but I fear we must empty several hundred of the cans of meat into the ocean. Hopefully we will be able to replace much of it with fresh meat. Mr. Gore is organizing the hunting. He's a good shot and should have some success, although I hear that the muskoxen hereabouts are difficult to stomach.

"Still," he continued, "all is not lost. We are well supplied despite the loss, and we can reuse the cans. The tin has many uses and we can melt the lead solder down for musket balls to supply the hunters with ammunition. But for now I must catch what rest I can."

I collected the soup bowl and spoon and left, wondering if the spoiled food might be a problem and what muskoxen tasted like. Since it was the first day for some time without cloud, I decided to take advantage and stretch my legs. I bundled up as well as possible and followed the line of posts to the shore of North Devon, the land to which Beechey Island is attached by a narrow isthmus.

I found myself in an unearthly landscape. The cliffs behind me loomed dark, like the walls of some fantastical fortress, but they served to block the bitter wind that blew eternally from the north in this desolate land. All else was white. Even the dark trails of the exercise paths around our vessels were bleached by a recent snowfall. The new snow blanketed the scene and made it impossible to tell where the sloping beach ended and the frozen water began. If it were not for the ships, tilted and black out in the bay, there would have been nothing to give the scene scale. It seemed almost that I could reach over and touch the shore of Beechey Island, even though it was more than a mile away.

I knew there were hollows and rises on the beach, but the landscape was so flat and white that I could not see them until I stumbled upon them. I had no plans for venturing farther — the chances of getting lost were too high.

But despite the cold nipping at my exposed skin, it was a joy to escape from the warm, damp, stinking atmosphere of the ship for an hour or two. It was good that the main deck of *Erebus* was heated, but with more than sixty unwashed, clay-pipe–smoking men in there, not to mention the burning candles and oil lamps, it sometimes seemed more like a foul pit.

As I stood and looked around, squinting to try to make out any features of interest, I noticed an odd lump in the snow some distance away. Wondering what it was, I made my way over.

When I was halfway to my destination, the mound moved. Shedding snow in a light, dry cloud, the largest creature I had ever seen reared up. It was a white bear. I watched in mounting horror as it continued rising until it stood near twice my height. The beast was pure white, with only the black of its nose, eyes and the pads on its massive forepaws showing.

I could not force my feet to move, and even if I could have, running would have been futile. Snow was this animal's natural habitat, and while the thick powder would only impede my stumbling progress, I had no doubt that the bear could lunge over to me in only a few strides. We stood and looked at each other, the bear curious, me terrified.

The beast took a few shuffling steps forward, its large, flat nose twitching at my scent. My heart beat so fast that I feared it was about to burst from my chest. I was breathing in short gulps and, despite the cold, sweat was breaking out on my palms.

The bear leaned forward until it rested on all fours, its face almost level with mine, and a mere 3 or 4 feet away. The head tilted from side to side as the beast examined me. As it did so, it let out a series of soft snuffling noises. Then the monster roared. A huge dark cavern lined with sharp yellow teeth, some as long as my finger, opened. A loathsome smell of rotting fish washed over me. My stomach lurched. I was convinced that my entire head was about to disappear into the disgusting jaws. I could almost feel flesh being torn from my skull and my bones being crushed by those powerful jaws. I think I whimpered in fear.

For what seemed like an eternity, we stood completely still, regarding one another. The bear was trying to work out what I was; I was thinking these were my final moments on earth.

I didn't recognize the explosion as a musket firing nearby. The bear reared up and threw its great head back. I cried out in terror, certain that I was about to be crushed by the weight of this mountainous form looming over me. However, the bear swung to one side of me.

As it did so, one of its massive forepaws caught me on the right shoulder. Had I not been wearing such a thick layer of clothing against the cold, the blow would have ripped my arm off. As it was, it knocked me some 10 feet across the beach, where I lay gasping. I was vaguely aware of a figure running towards me and of the huge bear lumbering off, before I passed out.

I came to in the sick bay of *Erebus,* with Surgeon Stanley fussing over me. "Good morning," he said cheerfully.

I attempted to sit up, but waves of pain in my shoulder forced me back.

"Quite the blow you took there, young man," Stanley informed me. "No bones are broken, but it will be some time before you lift a cup of rum with that arm. You'll have a bruise to be proud of in a day or so."

I looked at my shoulder, which Stanley had uncovered. A livid, deep-red mark spread over the joint and was already working its way down my arm. "What happened?" I asked.

"It seems you met one of the great white bears that inhabit these regions. Lucky for you that you weren't alone." Stanley nodded to the sick-bay door.

With an effort, I turned my head to see Davy leaning against the door jamb. "What happened?" I repeated.

"Was out hunting for some fresh meat, Georgie boy," Davy said casually. "Come down this gully and saw your bear. Took a shot. Missed the head, but hit the shoulder, looks like. There were blood splashes on the snow."

"You saved my life once more, Davy," I said. "Thank you."

Davy shrugged. "Bear got away afore I could reload," he went on, ignoring my thanks. "Pity. Could've used some of that fresh meat." With a wink, he turned and disappeared along the deck.

Chapter 7
New Year
Beechey Island, 1846

We began 1846 full of hope and celebrated with a ball on the frozen ocean. A large rectangle of ice, cleared and smoothed and surrounded by a low wall, defined the "ballroom." The crew stood around the wall, which was decorated with various fluttering flags and along which oil torches blazed to dispel the dark. At one end of the ballroom, Sir John sat imperiously on a magnificent ice-carved throne beneath a sign that read *Hope for the New Year*. At the other end, Sinclair, who had taught Davy and me how to work on the rigging, laboured to force a wailing tune from a set of bagpipes. Beside him, a seaman pounded enthusiastically on a set of makeshift drums.

In the centre of the rectangle, Mr. Fitzjames was dancing with Lieutenant Fairholme. They were ridiculous, cumbersome figures, wearing such bulky protection against the bitter cold and stumbling about like two mythical beasts locked in combat. Mr. Fairholme wore a crudely stitched green ball gown over his clothing. Much to the amusement of all, both the officers were having considerable difficulty deciding who should lead.

The marine, William Braine, stood beside me. We had become friends since I'd told him Father's story of the *Billy Ruffian* at Trafalgar.

"This is a strange world and no mistake," Braine commented as he busied himself with his clay pipe. "Are you glad you signed on for this adventure?"

"Of course I am," I replied. "I have seen wonders I could not even dream about before — ice tens of feet thick, moving, creaking and growling like a living creature; and dancing lights at midnight swirling across the sky and bright enough to read by."

William nodded as he lit his pipe. He drew long on it and was overcome by violent coughing.

"Are you sick?" I asked as the fit subsided.

"No more than I've been for many a year," William replied, wiping his eyes. "My lungs've always been weak, since I was a child. I had hopes that the cold up here might do them good, but it seems not."

I considered suggesting that the foul-smelling tobacco he stuffed in the pipe that eternally stuck out from his lips didn't help his cough, but it would have done no good. Pipes were universal among the crew, and the air below decks permanently thick with smoke.

"Take care," I said, "or you'll end up like John Hartnell, trapped in Surgeon Stanley's sick bay for weeks, and getting no better, they say."

"Aye," William agreed, "though I hear Torrington on *Terror*'s worse." Braine tapped the contents of his pipe out on his boot. "Word is that he's sinking and he'll not see many more days, let alone home. Idiot."

"Idiot? Surely it's not his fault that he has fallen sick."

"The word from my mates over there is that he has the consumption and was coughing blood long before he ever went to sick bay. Must have known he was bringing sickness aboard when he signed on."

"Surgeon Peddie will do the best he can," I said, not wanting to believe we were about to lose one of our party.

"I daresay." William shrugged and stamped his feet on the ice. "Sometimes I think none of us were meant to come to this harsh land."

"But we have overcome the harshness with our inventions," I said.

"So our choices are to sit and sweat in a stinking

ship's hold or freeze to death out in the darkness. I'd rather there was a war to fight. Then at least I could do what I was trained to do.

"But pay no attention to my griping. It's just the boredom and this eternal darkness that's getting to me — same as everyone else. Boredom's the worst thing you can inflict on a soldier or a sailor. Most would rather be wounded in battle than sit with nothing to do for months on end. I can't wait for the sun to come back so I can talk my way onto one of those exploring parties. It's brutal hauling those sleds, but I've never feared hard work. At least we have beer tonight, and I think I'll get me some before it freezes."

William headed off towards a group of men clustered around a fire on the ice, where quartermaster John Downing was tapping a large beer barrel and filling the men's cups.

"It's good to see the high and mighty officers making fools of themselves," said a voice beside me.

I turned to see that Davy had joined me. "Surely this is better than lying stinking in your hammock?" I rejoined.

"Well, the beer's good and I had a laugh at those idiots cavorting about out there." Davy's voice sounded scornful and mean.

"That's not fair," I said, more loudly than I had intended. The thought that Mr. Fitzjames and Mr. Fairholme looked silly had crossed my mind, but I didn't like Davy saying it, or the way he said it. "The officers have worked hard to keep boredom at bay, and boredom will cause trouble," I said, remembering what William had told me. "If you don't like this, there is to be a theatrical performance later this month."

"A *theatrical* performance," Davy scoffed. I smelled rum on his breath. "More excuses to dress up in stupid clothing. There's more theatre on the streets of Whitechapel than any of these upper-class gentlemen could ever imagine. Their lives are boredom. What work do the officers ever do? Who smoothed the ice for this? *We* did, the common sailors. We do everything. All the officers do is sit around, drink wine and discuss the fancy lives they'll lead when they return home rich and famous, while we wait on them hand and foot. Look at that idiot Fairholme dressed like a street woman and cavorting with your favourite officer."

"You're being too harsh," I said, my anger rising even more because I had also thought it funny that Mr. Fairholme had looked like a street woman. "Mr. Fitzjames has always treated me well and he works hard on the magnetic readings."

"Magnetic readings are about as much use as that book learning you're so fond of," Davy shot back. "I thought you had some sense, Georgie, but you've been taken in by a few kind words from an officer. Fitzjames and the others ain't about to care for the likes of you and me. They'd leave us to freeze in an instant if it'd help them. You've a lot to learn about the world. The only good thing the officers have done so far is open a cask of beer for the sailors, and I aim to make sure I get my share."

He moved past me and pushed his way though the crowd to the beer barrel. I was debating whether to follow him to continue our argument, but my anger vanished when I saw Surgeon Peddie approaching from *Terror*. A cold sense of foreboding, which had nothing to do with the thermometer, swept over me as he walked rapidly up to Sir John and whispered in his ear.

Several sailors also noticed Peddie's arrival and some men stopped their cavorting and watched. As attention focused on Sir John, Sinclair's bagpipes wailed into silence and the drums ceased. Sir John looked about for a moment and then stood. "I would have wished to keep the news I have just heard," he said. "But I see that it must intrude on our celebrations. Surgeon Peddie informs me that John Torrington, Leading Stoker aboard HMS *Terror*, passed on to a better world not a half hour past."

Sir John paused as a murmur ran through the crowd. "It is unfortunate," he continued, "that one so young should have succumbed to illness so early in our noble venture, but it is God's will. I am informed that Torrington's lungs have long been weak. He should not have concealed this fact when he signed up. Nevertheless, we shall bury him with due ceremony and his grave shall remain here as an eternal memorial to the sacrifice that is the cost of our noble endeavours. Meanwhile, we must look forward to the glory we have yet to achieve."

As soon as Sir John sat back down, a babble of voices broke out across the ice. All optimism seemed to vanish.

I moved to the beer barrel, where Davy and the old sailor, Bill, were talking.

"It be a bad omen," Bill said. "A death so early on."

"Two deaths," Davy added.

"What do you mean, two?" I asked.

"I reckon John Hartnell will not be long joining Torrington in the ground," Davy said, looking at me.

"Bad omen," Bill repeated. "No good'll come of this, you mark my words."

"That's nonsense," I blurted out, annoyed by

his miserable tone. "Torrington should never have come on the expedition. He had weak lungs and kept it secret. Surgeon Peddie did all he could, feeding him the best canned food and giving him the best care. It's stupid to say that Torrington's death is an omen — it has nothing to do with the expedition's success."

Bill coughed and spat onto the ice. "Aye, that's as may be," he said, "but there's many a man aboard these ships with lungs no better than Torrington and Hartnell. Are they all to die afore we get home?" Muttering "Bad omen," he moved away.

A memory of William Braine's violent cough flashed through my mind, but I pushed it away. "It's nonsense," I repeated, hoping that Davy would agree with me. Instead he simply laughed, and turned back to the beer barrel.

Three days later we buried John Torrington in the frozen ground of Beechey Island. We returned to the ship to find that John Hartnell was dead.

Chapter 8
The First Winter

Beechey Island, Early 1846

Despite us being secure, warm and well-fed in our sheltered bay at Beechey Island, the mood remained low after Torrington's and Hartnell's deaths. Parry and Ross had spent years in this land without a casualty. We had lost two men in our first winter. Part of the problem was the boredom, which gave everyone too much time to dwell on how far we were from help should anything go wrong.

I had never imagined that having nothing to do could be such a crushing burden. The minutes dragged like hours, the hours like days and the days like months. Men became listless and stood at the rail staring at the horizon, as if willing the sun to return and break the eternal darkness that blanketed us. Without any distinction between day and night, it was possible to imagine that time had stopped and that we were locked in some magical, never-changing limbo of ice and snow.

The officers did their best, running classes in

everything from reading and writing to navigation and history. Mr. Fitzjames organized a series of talks by the officers on their adventures. He himself addressed us a number of times on his experiences in the recent war in China. He was a very entertaining speaker, even including episodes from an epic poem he had written about the Chinese war. I attended everything I could, but many, like Bill, preferred to find solace in gambling, grumbling and drinking. During one performance of *Macbeth*, which the entire crew was obliged to attend, Bill became so loud as a consequence of drink that he had to be removed and held in irons until sober.

Davy began spending more and more time with Bill and the others while I found solace with Neptune, spending many pleasant hours huddled beside him on the deck, sharing my joys and fears, shivering and wishing I could be as unaffected by the cold as he was. He was the perfect audience, listening endlessly as long as I kept scratching him behind his ears.

Neptune was not the only animal on board. Jacko was a small monkey that had been brought aboard as the crew's mascot. He was dressed in a tiny suit of sailor's clothes and allowed free run of the deck and rigging. Many thought him an amusing distraction and applauded his wild antics. In truth, Jacko was more of a pest, stealing anything that caught his fancy and disappearing up to the highest yard with it.

"One day that beast'll be found with its neck broke," Bill said after Jacko had stolen his pipe and broken it by dropping it from the mast.

In March, Bill, Davy and I were sent below the main deck among the stores to check on Bill's rat traps. In the warm vessel with plenty of food on hand, the rats had bred quickly and become quite a problem. They were everywhere, scuttling across the decking, gnawing their way through any supplies not secured in cans or solid casks. They were large, fearless and dangerous. I had been woken several times by the feel of tiny, sharp feet running over me in the night. One man had even wakened after falling asleep on the deck to find a rat busily gnawing on his finger.

"That Jacko's a damn nuisance," Bill grumbled.

"It were just a clay pipe," Davy said to him. "You got others."

Bill hauled a barrel of flour aside to uncover one of his traps. A black rat looked up at us, held by a thin wire around its neck. It must have struggled to escape, as the fur around the wire was caked with dried blood. Bill lifted his club and brought it down twice on the rat's head. "There's too many of them to deal with by traps," he said as Davy untangled the rat's corpse from the wire. "We need to poison 'em."

"How can we do that?" I asked. "We can't spread poison amongst the food." I didn't enjoy helping Bill with rat catching, but he had been assigned the task after his drunken display during the play, and Davy and I had been ordered to help him.

"Arsenic and sulphur's the way, ain't that right, Bill?" Davy said. He enjoyed these expeditions much more than I did, and I had been surprised several times at how much he knew about rat catching.

"That's the way," Bill agreed. "Burn buckets of arsenic and sulphur through the ship. The fumes'll get the rats, but they don't taint the food. Won't get all the rats, mind, but it'll keep them down for a while. Trouble is, you can't eat them if they're poisoned."

"*Eat* them," I asked.

Davy laughed and swung the rat's bloodstained carcass by its tail. "Not a lot of meat on them and they're tough enough, but you boil a few of them in a stew kettle and they ain't too bad."

"I've eaten worse," Bill said, and I shuddered at the thought of what might be worse than boiled rat. He looked up from resetting his trap and saw my look of disgust. "After another year of salt pork and mouldy biscuits, I reckon even you'll find a bit of fresh rat a delicacy."

The following day, the weather being the mildest for some time, the entire crew not occupied at either the magnetic camp or the onshore building were assembled on the ice as Bill and a couple of others set buckets of arsenic and sulphur alight between decks. While we shivered, grey smoke issued from the ship. Even at some distance, the acrid smell caught the backs of many throats. I wondered how anything on board could survive.

After the buckets burned out, Davy and I were part of the crew ordered to remove the dead rats. Most had run out onto the open deck to try to escape, and so the bodies were easy to pick up. There were soon almost two hundred carcasses laid out beside the ship.

I was down amongst the stores with Davy and Bill, searching for the last few hidden bodies. It was unpleasant work, with the choking smell of the poison lingering in the air, but there was worse. I pulled aside a barrel and saw what I assumed was another rat carcass. I wasn't concentrating — otherwise I would have seen the dark blue material. I reached down and pulled up Jacko's limp form. His long limbs dangled oddly and his tiny face was distorted into such an expression of horror and agony that I dropped the body, stepped back and gasped.

"What you found there?" Bill asked.

"It's Jacko," I managed to reply.

"Serves him right," Bill said. "Probably planning some mischief and didn't get out in time. Won't be many misses him."

I looked up in time to catch Bill winking at Davy.

"It's just a monkey," Davy said when he saw my expression.

Yes, Jacko was just a monkey, but I left the hold convinced that his death hadn't been an accident. No one, not even a monkey, deserved that end.

After the Jacko incident, I tried to avoid Bill and Davy, but it was impossible in the narrow confines of the ship. Anyway, I had to admit that I missed Davy's stories. I knew now of my friend's dark side, and we no longer had the easy relationship of our early days together in Woolwich, but I still envied his confidence and devil-may-care attitude. His stories of hair-raising escapes and a life of petty theft on the London streets, always just one step ahead of the Peelers, fascinated me and went some way to relieving the winter boredom.

I understood Davy's life better now that I was more familiar with the rougher elements of society — people such as Bill. I didn't put Davy in the same category as Bill, but I did resent that he was increasingly spending time with the likes of the old sailor and his rough cronies, gambling at crown-and-anchor and drinking rum. More and more I spent time with William, talking of his adventures in the Navy, or confiding my worries to Neptune. I also came to know Mr. Fitzjames better, and even Sir John occasionally deigned to converse with a lowly cabin boy.

Every Sunday Sir John led a church service on deck. During these, he often talked of the importance of what we were engaged in and how our endeavour matched the great achievements of Parry and Ross. He was a very religious man and utterly convinced that God was on our side and smiling upon our work. He even agreed — at Mr. Fitzjames's urging, I suspect — to spend an evening telling us tales of his adventures on the Coppermine River. Of course, I knew of poor Lieutenant Hood slowly starving to death because he could not stomach the lichen that they scraped off the rocks to eat; of Dr. Richardson being forced to shoot the *voyageur* that he suspected of plotting to kill them for food; and of Mr. Back's heroic journey to find help, but it was a particular thrill to hear the tales from the mouth of The Man Who Ate His Boots himself.

One day, as the hours of sunshine lengthened and the weather warmed, I was clearing away the dinner dishes for Sir John and Mr. Fitzjames in the Great Cabin.

"Well, young man," Sir John said to me as the two men sat back to enjoy a glass of port. "How have you enjoyed your first year as a sailor?"

"Very much, sir," I said, nervous as I always was on the rare occasions when the great man spoke to me.

"Do you remember when you approached me on the dock at Woolwich?" Mr. Fitzjames asked.

"Very well, sir," I said. "It seems like only yesterday."

Mr. Fitzjames chuckled and Sir John asked, "So the boredom of inactivity does not trouble you?"

"It does a bit, sir, but my clerk's desk was boring as well and I never came face to face with a great white bear in Woolwich."

Sir John laughed. "Well said. You were lucky to survive the encounter, I hear."

"I was, sir."

"Good lad." Sir John was in a jovial mood, his cheeks glowing from the warmth, good food and wine. "You come from a naval family. Do you plan a future in the service?"

"Yes, sir," I said, although in truth I was by no means so certain.

"Well, I owe your father a great debt. Had he not bayonetted that Frenchman on the old *Billy Ruffian*, I should not be here now in charge of the greatest expedition ever to leave England's shores." Sir John paused for a moment. "Or had the chance to eat my boots."

Sir John and Mr. Fitzjames guffawed and I joined in nervously. "In any case" — Sir John wiped his face and went on — "I shall be glad to provide a reference and a quiet word in an important ear should you require it."

"Thank you very much, sir. It's an honour to serve with you." Since Sir John was being so talkative, I was bold enough to ask a question that had been on my mind for some time. "When can we expect the ice to release us, sir?"

"That's a question we would all like answered," Sir John said, "although I suspect it's one only God knows the answer to. Certainly not for some months yet. What is your opinion, James?"

Mr. Fitzjames sucked his teeth thoughtfully for a moment. "Perhaps in June if this mild weather continues. Our exploring parties are certainly out much earlier than we could expect, according to Parry and Ross's journals."

"Will Mr. Gore's party be back soon?" I asked. William had joined the exploration party heading east along the coast of North Devon. He had been gone some time and I looked forward to his return. Friendship with William was much less complicated than with Davy and I'd grown fond of the gruff marine and his stories.

"Any day now if they haven't run into difficulties," Mr. Fitzjames said.

"Will we complete the Passage this summer, sir?" I asked, encouraged by the relaxed atmosphere.

"I think we shall. God willing, of course," Sir John answered. "Mr. Fitzjames, do you agree that the channel to the south that Mr. Gore discovered last autumn, and which was so kindly named after my dear wife Jane, will provide the route we seek?"

"I think Lady Jane Franklin Strait will lead us in exactly the right direction, sir," Mr. Fitzjames replied. "However, it is so narrow that I fear it will not open until late in the season."

"No matter." Sir John waved a hand dismissively. "We shall spend our time exploring Wellington Channel. It appears to head some distance north and might connect to an open ocean in that direction. I do not personally hold with that idea, but we will add more lines to the chart. Then when my wife's strait clears of ice, we shall head south, complete the Passage and head for home."

He turned from Mr. Fitzjames to me. "Are you eager for home yet, young George?"

"I am eager for the warm lands of the Sandwich Islands," I said with a smile.

"Indeed," Sir John said. "I am as well, although I do not think Mr. Fitzjames will be joining us there."

I looked up at Mr. Fitzjames.

When he saw my puzzled expression, he said, "I have requested, and Sir John has kindly agreed, that I and a small party be put off on the shores of Russia. We will return home overland. It will be a wonderful adventure and I shall be back in London with our great news before the ships arrive."

"May I come with you?" I blurted out. Both men laughed. "I'm sorry," I apologized. "That was unforgivably presumptuous of me."

"No. No," Mr. Fitzjames said hurriedly. "In fact, I have had thoughts along similar lines. You are an intelligent boy and would be of use in my venture. I am sure I can arrange it." He looked at Sir John.

"Of course," Sir John said, "although you will be depriving me of a fine servant."

"Thank you," I said.

"But we must complete *this* task first," Sir John continued. "And to do that, we — "

"Sled returning!"

A shouted voice from the deck above cut short our conversation.

We hurried out on deck and peered over the rail into the Arctic twilight. The sled was already close to the ship. It was coming from the east, so it had to be Mr. Gore's exploration team. I was happy that William was back and looked forward to the tales he would have.

At first all I could see were bundled, hunched figures straining forward against the weight of the sled, which was piled high with supplies, tent, stove and sleeping sacks.

"They're one short," Mr. Fitzjames said.

I hurriedly counted the toiling figures — seven. The hauling team had set out eight strong. Something had gone wrong.

Men clambered over the side of the ship to help their comrades. It was only when the sled was man-oeuvred alongside that I saw a frozen body atop it, and only when the body was brought aboard that I recognized it as that of William Braine.

"Oh no," I gasped.

William looked peaceful but horribly thin.

His body was frozen solid, like a statue carved in impossibly white stone.

"Take him down to the sick bay," Surgeon Stanley ordered. "We will prepare him for burial there."

I watched as my friend's corpse was man-handled down the hatch. I couldn't stop the tears.

"He was your friend, the marine?" Mr. Fitzjames asked.

"Yes, sir," I replied. "I warned him not to go. I said he could beg off the exploration party. He had been losing weight and his cough was getting worse. He shouldn't have gone."

"Don't blame yourself," Mr. Fitzjames said. "I'm sure he knew what he was doing."

A bundled figure approached and stood in front of us. "A sad event, Mr. Gore," Sir John said.

"Indeed, sir," Mr. Gore agreed. "Braine collapsed when we were at our farthest from the ships. He was coughing blood. I can't imagine how he managed to get so far. In any case, it was obvious he couldn't go on. We camped and he lay delirious for three days, after which we were trapped for a further three by a blizzard. We returned with all haste."

"Very good, Mr. Gore," Sir John said. "See to the care of yourself and your men. You can report fully to me later."

It was hard getting over William's death. His Royal Marine companions took great care over his burial, allowing me to stamp out the details of his sad fate on the copper plaque affixed to the coffin lid. We had to work fast. When we brought his body on board to the warmth, it rapidly became obvious that his remains were not in the best condition. That and the attention of the rats to his body gave us good reason to work fast. Nevertheless, we took care, dressed him in his best clothes and laid his favourite red kerchief over his face.

We buried him deep, beside Torrington and Hartnell. Another grave.

It was a sad trilogy of headstones that marked our sojourn at Beechey Island, and although there were good times and optimism after that spring of 1846, there was also a horrible inevitability to every event. It seemed that nothing we attempted completely succeeded. I tried to remain optimistic, but as the weeks wore on, I began to see us as mere toys at the whim of a cruel and uncaring nature.

Davy was no help to me in my sorrow after William died. "Should never have gone off sled hauling," he commented. "Won't catch *me* doing that if I can help it. It's brutal work."

I continued to avoid Davy and his gambling friends. I spent more time with Neptune. His friendship was unconditional and I could tell him all my worries without fear of some harsh comment.

Chapter 9
Hope Destroyed
King William Island, 1846–1847

As Mr. Fitzjames had predicted, spring came early and mild that year of 1846. When the ice released us in early July, we sailed up Wellington Channel in search of open water. The going was slow. Leads opened and closed around us, forcing us to go where they led. Our steam engine grumbled and hissed and kept our engineer, John Gregory, busy when it broke at the most inconvenient times.

When it did, everyone piled onto the ice and man-hauled the ships forward. At other times, we had to break out the ice saws and cut our way through to open water. It was many weeks' work to progress the 150 miles north up Wellington Channel, but it was most welcome after the boredom of our enforced winter idleness.

On August 6 we were finally beset at 77 degrees north. We lingered for some days at this northerly point for Mr. Fitzjames to take magnetic readings. While doing so, many of the crew climbed a nearby hill to gaze upon what some had thought would be open ocean. It was not. The first time I gazed upon that scene, it was with horror. As far as the eye could see, huge slabs of ice, some greater than 10 or 12 feet in thickness, lay tossed about at all angles, like the discarded playthings of some giant impetuous child. The power of nature to create such a mountain range of ice left me speechless. How could we possibly manage if these forces were turned against us?

The way back south was uneventful and we crossed over to Lady Jane Franklin Strait without difficulty. The strait was open, restoring our confidence, and we sailed down with lighter hearts, thinking God was offering us easy passage. It was only later that we recognized it as a temptation of the devil.

In September we arrived at the north end of King William Island. As there was no way down either coast — the east side being too shallow for our draft and the west too ice-clogged — we prepared for our second winter. With no safe land harbour, we cut docks into a large, stable slab of several-year-old ice and linked our location to a camp at Cape Felix, the most northerly tip of King William Island, by a trail over the ice.

The mood was low. However, we were convinced we were faced with only one final hurdle that we would overcome with ease in the summer of 1847 and be through to Bering's Strait and the warm Pacific Ocean before that year was out.

We lay at the limits of the known world. A few miles south of Cape Felix lay Victory Point, named by James Ross when he reached his farthest distance west in 1830. On the south shore of King William Island, a mere 60 miles south of Victory Point, was the cairn at Cape Herschel built by Simpson and Dease in 1839. All we needed to do was traverse that 60 miles from Victory Point to Cape Herschel and we could claim everlasting fame as the discoverers of the Northwest Passage.

Not being on land, the winter of 1846–1847 was harder than our time at Beechey Island. A magnetic camp was established at Cape Felix, but it was a hard journey over rough and continually changing ice to get there. On board ship the officers organized theatricals and lessons in the arts and sciences, Sir John encouraged us with his Sunday sermons, and Bill hunted rats, griped and complained. Davy gambled and drank more than before and was prone to fits of sudden anger. I spent more time with faithful Neptune, repeating the stories my father, William Braine and Davy had told me.

Just as we were beginning to see a few hours of

daylight each day, two men died: Josephus Geater of a mysterious illness that baffled both Surgeon Stanley and Mr. Goodsir; and Thomas Tadman in a fall from the bowsprit onto the ice. Davy merely commented that Tadman was drunk, which may have been true.

My boredom that winter was eased by being assigned to help Mr. Gore build and modify our sleds for the coming spring explorations. "Different sleds for different purposes," Mr. Gore used to say. "The Hudson Bay men and the Esquimaux use light dog-drawn sleds. Fast, but no use for scientific work where you need to carry equipment and samples of what you find. That requires larger vehicles, and it is our goal, young George, to create a sled big enough for our scientific work, but not so heavy that the men hauling it will break down from the strain."

Mr. Gore was always tinkering, shaving down a support here, modifying a runner there. He talked continually as we worked, sometimes to me, sometimes to himself and sometimes to the sled. "Our task would be easier if we simply had to travel over flat ice, but hauling over these damnable ridges puts such a strain on the sled frame. Hold that beam there young George while I hammer this nail in." I did as he ordered. "There, that's a good boy," he added, patting his finished work — all Mr. Gore's sleds seemed to be male. "Now you're much lighter."

As May drew on, Mr. Gore was selected to lead a party consisting of Mr. Des Voeux and six men down the west coast of King William Island to Cape Herschel. He was to have the honour of completing the Northwest Passage and fulfilling a dream that had propelled men into these unforgiving lands since the days of Frobisher and Hudson.

While Mr. Gore headed for glory, Lieutenant Little and Mr. Hornby were to take a second sled down the east side of King William Island. Their task would also be important, proving whether or not King William Island was attached to the land to the east. It was hoped the two parties would meet on the south shore of the island, perhaps even at Cape Herschel itself.

Mr. Fitzjames prepared messages giving our position and a brief history of our doings so far, for the explorers to place in tin cans under piles of stones as they progressed. The plan was for both parties to first head for the magnetic camp at Cape Felix. From there, Lieutenant Little was to head down the east coast of King William Island and Mr. Gore down the west.

On May 24 the two sleds were seen off with much fanfare, good wishes and cheering. Sir John, although he had been unwell and confined to his cabin for several days, came on deck and made a speech befitting the historic moment. He said that Gore and Little would be forging a vital link in the chain that bound our great empire together.

Each sled had been christened and its name emblazoned on a handmade flag that fluttered from a pole at the stern. To my delight, Mr. Little had chosen *Bellerophon*, the warrior after whom my father's ship had been named. Mr. Gore had selected *Orion*, the hunter.

I stood at the rail watching those laden men struggling to haul their burdens over the ice until they were mere tiny dots. By then most of the rest of the crew had returned to their duties. The only other group nearby were Davy and his friends.

"Do you wish you were going with them?" I asked Davy.

"Why would I wish to be working like a slave when I can be cozy and warm here on board ship?"

"For the *adventure*," I said. "The excitement. The glory of completing the Northwest Passage."

"Glory?" Davy muttered. "Ain't no glory in working yourself to death tied to hundreds of pounds of useless equipment. The glory's in the fame and fortune that awaits us when we return home. Then you'll hear stories about what I done here that'll make what them officers're doing look like a Sunday walk in the park." Davy waved his arm at the horizon where the two groups of slowly receding figures were still occasionally visible amongst the ice.

I was shocked at his cynical attitude. How could his heart not soar at what we were achieving?

"We should be turning for home," Bill said.

"Home?" I exclaimed.

"Aye, home. Ain't no way through this damned ice. This ain't no place fer God-fearing men."

"It's as well you're not God-fearing, then," Davy said with a laugh. Bill grunted and fell silent.

"We can't go home," I said. "That would be a failure. As soon as the ice releases us, we must head west and complete sailing through the Passage."

Bill snorted at that.

"You have to admire young Georgie's optimism," Davy pointed out. "If he were in a prison cell, he'd spend half a day hammering on the locked door before turning and saying, 'Oh well. No matter. I ain't tried the barred window yet.'"

Several men laughed and I felt my face flush. "You don't deserve to be heroes of the Northwest Passage," I shouted. "You're nothing but cowards."

I meant the words for Bill and the others, but anger flashed in Davy's eyes. He spun to face me, his mouth twisted. "Call me a coward again and you'll feel my blade through your ribs," he growled. Then he stalked off.

I looked after him, shocked at the violence in his tone.

Bill chuckled quietly. "Best not to annoy yer young friend," he advised. "He don't take kindly to being called names."

I stumbled away. Someone made a comment I couldn't hear, but the men laughed and I knew it was directed at me. I went in search of Neptune to tell him my worries.

In the succeeding days, I worked even harder at avoiding Davy, but it was impossible. Oddly, when next I bumped into him, he was his usual cheery self. "Think nothing of it, Georgie boy," he said. "Too much salt pork makes me miserable." It was as if he had completely forgotten laughing at me and then threatening me with his knife.

As the days passed, and the return of our explorers neared — the conquerors of the Northwest Passage as we already thought of them — excitement rose. The weather remained fair and we assumed that they must be making good time. In spare moments, some of the sailors would

97

wander to the rail and gaze off in the direction that Mr. Gore and Mr. Little would appear from. Everyone wanted to be the first to spot them.

On June 11 I was standing at the rail with Neptune as his tail thumped happily on the deck, when Mr. Fitzjames appeared beside me. "Any sign of our warriors returning?" he asked.

"Not yet, sir, but it cannot be long now. The weather has not been unduly harsh, so they should have made good time."

"Indeed they should, but the weather is not the only handicap. Who knows what they may have encountered to slow them. We are, after all, in unknown lands."

"But it will no longer be unknown when Mr. Gore returns," I said. "Will we make Bering's Strait by summer's end?"

Mr. Fitzjames smiled. "A year past you asked me a similar question."

"And you did not answer me," I ventured to remind him.

"I do not like predicting the future. It is too easy for life to make a fool of you. But yes, I am optimistic that as soon as this damnable ice releases us, we shall make good progress westward. Are you still game to accompany me on my adventure across Russia?"

"I am looking forward to it," I said. "Are you eager to see your family once more?"

"Such as it is," Mr. Fitzjames said. He looked at me thoughtfully for a minute. "You are lucky to have two loving parents and sisters and brothers."

"Your parents are no longer alive?"

"My father died the year before we sailed. As for my mother, I cannot say."

Mr. Fitzjames must have noticed my puzzled expression. "It is not so complicated, young George. My father was a well-known figure — you would recognize his name were I to say it — but his wife is not my mother."

He nodded and smiled at my gradually dawning realization. "Born out of wedlock," he said lightly. "Such a scandal. I was fostered out and the story that I had been orphaned was put about to explain things. Not that I should complain. My new family were as good as any man could ask for. Still and all, I sometimes wonder what a true family is like."

"I'm sorry," I said.

"Do not be. There have been difficult times, and I must take care who I tell as I rise through the Navy's ranks. Those in power are happy to believe that I was orphaned by the fever when I was a lad of seven. Look where I am now, an exalted captain on a famous expedition, and when I return across

Russia and arrive in England before the ships, I shall be even more famous. Perhaps then, no one will care who my parents were." Mr. Fitzjames laughed. "How odd this place makes us," he added. "I have spent my life hiding my parentage, and here I am blurting it to you. Still, I doubt you will find many to tell my secret in this land."

We were interrupted by a commotion behind us. We turned to see Sir John standing on the deck outside his cabin. He had remained unwell and mostly confined to his cabin after Mr. Gore and the others left.

My first reaction was joy that he must be feeling better, but he didn't look well. He had lost a lot of weight and his uniform jacket, unbuttoned despite the cold, hung loosely on his frame. He was hatless, his cheeks appeared sunken, and there was a pale, waxy sheen to his skin.

As we watched, Sir John took two uncertain steps. Mr. Fitzjames moved forward. Sir John stretched his right arm out, seeking something to steady himself. A puzzled expression crossed his face, as if he were having trouble focussing. Every man on deck fell silent and stared.

"Are you feeling better, sir?" Mr. Fitzjames asked.

Sir John turned his face towards us, his frown

deepening. He opened his mouth as if to speak, but nothing came out. Mr. Fitzjames was reaching out to help his commander when Sir John exhaled loudly and collapsed onto the deck as if his bones had turned to water. Neptune barked loudly and several sailors, myself included, rushed forward and carried our leader back into his cabin and laid him on his bunk. His eyes flickered open and his breathing came in shallow, rasping gasps.

Surgeon Stanley bustled in and ordered us all to leave. Two hours later, Captain Crozier arrived from *Terror* and he and Mr. Fitzjames announced to the assembled ships' companies that Sir John Franklin was dead.

We buried our leader with much ceremony on a high rise inland from the Cape Felix camp. It was as if the heart had been torn from our expedition. Even Bill and Davy could find nothing cynical to say. Captain Crozier, our new commander, and Mr. Fitzjames did their best to sound positive and hopeful, but a sense of deep foreboding settled over us all. As if in sympathy, the sky darkened steadily as we plodded back to the ships. By midnight we were in the grip of the worst blizzard we had ever experienced. We settled in to wait it out, increasingly worried about the exploration parties and the men isolated at the Cape Felix magnetic camp.

Chapter 10
The First Horror
King William Island, 1847

The blizzard raged for a full six days, while temperatures fell so far that the mercury in the thermometers solidified, and exposed flesh froze in minutes. It was impossible to step onto the ship's deck, let alone venture far over the ice. Ice crystals, blown in the teeth of a ferocious gale like shot from a gun, cut frozen skin to shreds. Snow often reduced visibility to less than an arm's length, buried the poles marking our paths across the ice and built up on the windward side of *Erebus*'s hull so high that it was possible to step over the rail onto firm drifts. The gale ripped the canvas shelters off the ships' open decks and snapped *Terror*'s foremast like a matchstick.

Waves of pressure, driven by wind and tide, rolled through the ice, thrusting great slabs of it into the air with terrifying screams. One launched itself skyward to the height of our foremast, and only scant yards away. While we huddled in fear that it would crash down upon us, it proved a blessing, remaining stationary and giving *Erebus* some protection from the incessant gale. Even the reinforced hulls of the ships creaked and groaned in protest. So many seams opened in *Terror*'s sides that the pumps had to be kept going continually. Preparations were made to abandon the ship.

As the storm drove on relentlessly, day after day, concern grew for those not on board ships and with inadequate protection against such vicious weather. On the sixth day, the blizzard ceased as suddenly as it had begun and the days turned mild and calm, as if nature had exhausted herself in the fury of the storm and needed rest. A new trail was blazed to Cape Felix, where the magnetic camp was found to be destroyed and the frozen bodies of Lieutenant Fairholme and Mate Edward Couch were discovered nearby, huddled together with the shreds of their canvas tent around them.

The discovery of their bodies emphasized the dire plight of the sixteen men of the exploration parties. On top of Sir John's loss, it was almost more than we could bear. Mr. Fitzjames got us busy organizing relief parties to scour King William Island for Gore and Little.

I petitioned Mr. Fitzjames ceaselessly to allow me to accompany him on one of the searches. Eventually he agreed, I think because I had worked on the sled design with Mr. Gore. Two sleds — one from *Erebus* and one from *Terror* — made their way to Cape Felix. We moved down the coast to Victory Point without finding any sign of our companions, so we established a camp while the sled from *Terror* returned to the ships to ferry more supplies ashore.

With a much-lightened sled, Mr. Fitzjames led four of us south at a fast pace. The going was easy as the June weather remained mild. We had 24 hours of daylight, and the flat land had not allowed the recent blizzard to form the snow into deep drifts. We had been travelling for some 10 hours, with only one break for rest and food, when Mr. Fitzjames, who was leading and some distance in front, stopped and shouted at us to throw off our harnesses, leave the sled and hurry forward.

We came upon a tragic scene. Six ragged, skeletal figures staggered towards us. It was an image from a nightmare, only made more unbelievable by occurring in bright sunshine.

Lieutenant Little led the pitiful group. He collapsed weeping into Mr. Fitzjames's arms. The rest of us rushed forward to help the others. All were in the last extremity of exhaustion. Their faces were blackened by frostbite and dirt; they hardly had the strength to stand. One man was so snow-blind from the glare of the sun on the white land that he had to be helped along by a companion.

We slowly made our way back to the sled, where we lit our crude stove and warmed some water for weak tea. Mr. Fitzjames ordered the wooden box sides from the sled to be broken up to build a fair-sized fire. The warmth and the sight of the flickering orange flames, combined with the lukewarm tea, biscuits and the simple knowledge of being rescued, enlivened the men remarkably. Haltingly, Mr. Little told their terrible story.

"The journey down the east coast went well," he began in a cracked voice that we all had to lean closer to hear. "It was hard work, but the weather was fine and we made good time. We managed to map the coast — proving that King William Island *is indeed* an island, distinctly separated from Boothia." A frown creased Mr. Little's forehead and he looked around in confusion. "I marked it on the chart," he said.

"Remember, sir," one of the men added. I recognized him as the marine, Joseph Healey — William Braine's friend. He was one of Mr. Gore's party. "We had to abandon the charts in the blizzard."

"Oh, yes," Little nodded, although he seemed rather uncertain, "so we did. A shame, because we mapped the coast."

"Yes, mapping is important," Mr. Fitzjames said gently. "Did you meet up with Mr. Gore at Cape Herschel then?"

"Yes. Yes." Mr. Little appeared encouraged and sipped his tea through cracked and blistered lips. "Mr. Gore's party awaited us at Cape Herschel. That was on . . . " Again the puzzled frown.

"The eleventh of June," Healey offered. He seemed the fittest of all.

"We celebrated," Mr. Little went on. "Mr. Gore had completed the Northwest Passage — forged the last link between Ross's Victory Point and Simpson and Dease's Cape Herschel. Mr. Gore will be famous."

Mr. Little's news should have had us cheering wildly — our great goal was achieved. But at such a frightful cost. And then the date struck me. How strange that the Passage had been completed on the very day of Sir John's death.

Eventually Mr. Little continued. "We were all tired from our exertions, and food was short. Mr. Des Voeux was injured."

"He slipped while hauling and a sled runner crushed his leg, sir." Healey filled in Mr. Little's silence. "Two days before we reached Cape Herschel. That's why we were still there when Mr. Little arrived. Mr. Des Voeux's leg was broke bad."

"Very bad," Mr. Little mumbled. "We moved as much of the supplies as we could onto our sled and strapped Mr. Des Voeux onto the other one. Mr. Gore was to take four men and travel fast with the light sled to get our injured companion back to the ships as fast as possible. We were to follow with the heavier load and the extra two men."

"Then the storm hit." Healey spoke when Mr. Little once more stopped talking. "We set up camp. It was crowded and we had scarce food, but we were more worried about Mr. Gore's party. They didn't have much with them. On the third day, the storm appeared to ease, so Mr. Hornby took three men and went to find Mr. Gore. I'm afraid we've not seen him since."

"But we found Mr. Gore," Mr. Little said distantly. "Dead though. All dead."

He drifted into silence once more and Healey took up the story. "They must have kept travelling in the blizzard," Healey said. "Not much choice, I suppose. The men were all together on a ridge, still harnessed to the sled, with Mr. Des Voeux on top. Frozen."

We all sat silently, staring at the flames before us. It was a tragedy we could barely comprehend. What should have been an inspiring triumph was a disaster that had cost the lives of ten men.

"If you are recovered enough," Mr. Fitzjames said eventually, "we must head back to the ships. I shall send out a party to bring in Mr. Gore and the others and to search for Mr. Hornby."

"Yes," Mr. Little said. "I must report all to Sir John."

"Mr. Crozier is in command now," Mr. Fitzjames told him. "I'm sorry to have to tell you that Sir John died on the day before the blizzard set in."

The men stared in silence. Even after what they had gone through, the news of Sir John's death was still powerful enough to shock them.

"How . . . How can we go on?" Mr. Little asked.

"Mr. Crozier will lead us," Mr. Fitzjames answered. "We shall take the ships through the Northwest Passage for Sir John."

The others nodded, but I did not see much conviction.

We reached the ships two days later and told our tragic tale. Mr. Gore and his companions' bodies were recovered. Mr. Hornby and his men were never found. In but a short while, we had gone from a successful expedition full of hope, to a leaderless, sadly depleted crew. The land that we had been exploring with such enthusiasm had become a cruel enemy, seemingly bent on our destruction.

Four days after we returned, Mr. Little sank into delirium, raving about home and talking to our dead companions as if they stood beside him. The following night he died.

Chapter 11
Visitors

King William Island, 1847

Neptune's wild barking from deck brought most of us to the ship's rail. It was August and one of the few days when the incessant fog that had surrounded us all year had lifted. The ice still held us firm, creaking and groaning all around, and we were worried that if it did not release us soon we would be facing another winter in this place, a prospect we dreaded.

The dark figures out on the ice were already getting near the ship by the time I arrived on deck and tried to calm Neptune. I counted nine in the party: four men, one of whom was of great age; three women; and two children. Neptune must have been upset by their small pack of skinny, noisy dogs that dragged a sled laden with furs and slabs of seal meat. Each man was dressed in animal hides, roughly sewn into long coats and loose leggings. Mr. Fitzjames went out onto the ice to meet them as they slowed and hesitated some distance away. After the presentation of gifts, all was smiles and our new companions swarmed aboard.

Mr. Crozier, who spoke some of the local language, arrived from *Terror*. We were all amazed to discover that our visitors knew of him from his journey to Prince Regent Inlet with Commander Parry many years before. They called Mr. Crozier Aglooka. He informed us that that was because he had exchanged names with a boy who was now called Crozar. Apparently this was a common habit among the people of this land.

The leader of the party was called Oonalee. He had had considerable contact with Europeans, so Mr. Crozier and Mr. Fitzjames took him in to the Great Cabin to pore over charts and drawings. The rest of the party remained on deck, where they soon attempted to steal anything that was not nailed down. They seemed to regard this as a great game and many of our crew entered into the spirit of it, but not all.

"Thieving savages," Davy muttered as he watched the antics.

I resisted the temptation to remind him of his own past life and simply remarked, "The people in this land have few of the luxuries we take for granted. A nail that they can turn into a fish hook or a spear point is a valuable item to them, and what is it to us?"

Davy grunted and changed the subject. "They stink," he said, "wearing animal skins all smeared with grease and fat."

"I wonder whether they think the same of us," I said, remembering the foul smell of sweat, filth and burning candles and oil lamps on the lower deck. "When did you last wash either yourself or your clothes?"

"That's different," Davy said, without explaining how. "They're savages."

"That may be, but they do live their entire lives in this land. I agree they would not do well in the streets of London, but perhaps had Mr. Gore and the others had these foul-smelling animal skins and dogs to draw their sleds this past spring, more of them might be alive now. Mr. Crozier thinks learning their language and ways important."

"Mr. Crozier and your other officer friends may go native if they wish. I shall hold with good old English ways."

Davy turned and stalked off. He didn't get far. He had recently taken to carrying his thin-bladed knife — the one he'd slid between Jim's ribs — tucked into his belt. Now, as he pushed through the throng on the deck, one of the natives slipped the knife out of Davy's belt and turned away.

"Hey!" Davy shouted. "Give that back, you filthy savage."

The man ignored the shouted command and made for the ship's side. Davy leaped after him, grabbing his loose coat as he made to climb over the rail. The pair fell to the deck and began struggling. Amidst much shouting and cursing, others, egged on by old Bill, joined the fray.

The scuffle was mostly noise and shoving, although Davy was swinging wild punches. The melee was threatening to degenerate into something much more serious when a musket shot froze everyone in place. Mr. Crozier and Mr. Fitzjames appeared from the cabin. Joseph Healey stood beside them, a smoking musket in his hand.

"What is the meaning of this?" Mr. Crozier demanded. "These people are our guests."

The crowd of sailors looked sheepish and slowly dispersed.

"That one stole my knife," Davy growled, pointing at the man he had attacked. He had retrieved his blade and stood holding it in front of him.

Mr. Crozier came forward. "These people live a harsh life in this land," he said. "A good knife blade is more valuable to them than a chest of gold would be to us. It is a sign of their peacefulness that they do not attempt to murder us in our sleep for our treasures. Now, you will exchange that knife for whatever this man feels is a fair price in seal meat."

"I will not," Davy said, holding the knife more threateningly.

"You will address a senior officer as sir," Mr. Crozier ordered calmly, "and you shall arrange a fair exchange with good grace, or I shall have you tied to the rigging and flogged. Do you understand?"

For a moment I wondered if Davy was about to do something stupid, but he merely grunted, "Aye. Aye, Sir," and dropped the knife to the deck.

"With good grace," Mr. Crozier repeated.

With an obvious effort, Davy retrieved the knife and offered it to the man who had attempted the theft. Mr. Crozier said something in the local language and the man nodded. He accepted the knife, retrieved a large, frozen hunk of seal meat and offered it to Davy. Davy took the meat and, without a word, turned and stalked across the deck. I think I was the only person who saw him drop the meat over the far rail.

Although the incident was smoothed over, our visitors insisted on leaving, despite Mr. Crozier's entreaties to stay and eat with us. They did not return.

"Would Mr. Crozier really have had Davy flogged?" I asked Mr. Fitzjames as I served him supper in his cabin.

"Undoubtedly."

"But I've heard the sailors talk of flogging. It sounds barbaric. I've heard a man's back can be stripped until his ribs are exposed. Men die of a flogging."

Mr. Fitzjames put down his pen and looked up at me. "Indeed it is barbaric, but many argue that it is necessary for discipline. We serve on a privileged ship, but think on this — there are near eight hundred men on a seventy-four–gun man-of-war, and many are from the gutters of the great port cities. The life on board during a long voyage, especially during war, is so brutal and dangerous that the captain must maintain discipline by having punishments that are worse than the sailors' daily life. Hence flogging before the assembled ship's company."

"But you said *Erebus* is a privileged ship and we are not at war," I pointed out.

"True enough, but we are not safe back in Woolwich either."

"And we might be facing another winter," I added, beginning to see where Mr. Fitzjames was going.

"Exactly. There have been too many deaths already. Spirits are low, and by next spring, if we have no luck hunting, we shall be short on food, thanks to the spoiled cans we lost. More seriously, we shall be perilously low on lemon juice."

"Scurvy?"

"A possibility, yes, and since the locals do not appear to suffer from scurvy, we can assume that there is something in their diet that prevents it. It may come down to our very lives depending upon good relations with the local inhabitants."

I had worried about several of the things Mr. Fitzjames talked about, but to have him state the situation so bluntly was shocking.

"But there are more than a hundred of us, sir," I said. "How can a few small bands of the locals possibly supply enough food, even if they are willing to help?"

Mr. Fitzjames's normally cheery face looked suddenly careworn and grim. "They can't," he said so quietly that I could barely hear him. "If the ice does not release us next summer, very few of us will be going home."

I couldn't believe what I was hearing. The greatest, best-prepared Arctic expedition in history, reduced to a few starving bands of men begging raw seal meat from the locals. It was impossible.

Mr. Fitzjames took a deep breath and his smile returned. "But listen to me croak on. You have found me downcast, George. Pay no attention to my griping. We have had bad luck, but the hunting will be good and the ice will release us next summer. You and I shall have our adventure across Russia, mark my words."

Chapter 12
Hope Rekindled
King William Island, 1848

That winter of 1847–1848 cast a long, dark shadow over me and everyone else. The sailors grumbled and complained, but what could anyone do? It was a cold, seemingly endless night, and we went about our tasks mechanically. It was as if we were surrounded by the wraiths of those who had already died. I often felt that, were I to glance over my shoulder, I would see Mr. Gore or William standing watching me.

We were trapped and dying, officers as well as men. By March of 1848, only 105 of our original complement of 129 were still alive, and the dreaded scurvy was running rampant. Mr. Crozier and Mr. Fitzjames talked long and hard in the Great Cabin and devised a desperate plan.

The surviving crews from both ships were gathered on the ice as Commander Crozier outlined his idea. "We shall take what supplies we can from *Terror* and store them onshore at Victory Point. *Terror*'s hull was much weakened by the ice last year and, should a lead of open water form beneath her, she will be on the bottom before we can return."

"*Return?*" A voice from the huddled mass of sailors shouted.

Mr. Crozier ignored it and continued. "It is early in the season to travel, especially for such a large group as ourselves, but we have no choice. Our food supplies are low, and even with rationing they will not last us all through this summer without supplement. More pressing, the rising cases of scurvy among us make the discovery of fresh food imperative.

"George Back, when he descended the Fish River, wrote of encountering much wildlife to the south of us, and this is confirmed by the journals of Simpson and Dease. We shall travel towards Back's Fish River, restock there and regain our strength. Then we shall return to the ships and complete our mission."

Mr. Crozier spoke plainly and in a clear tone, but he did not have Sir John's ability to inspire us. A murmur of grumbling began to arise from the men around me. Eventually a voice shouted out, "If we come back here we die." A mumble of agreement rolled through the crowd.

Mr. Fitzjames stepped forward. "Who said that?" There was no response.

"You will not be punished for speaking up," Mr. Crozier said, "but you must step forward."

There was a commotion nearby and Bill stepped out from the crowd. "Begging your pardon, sir," he began. "But some of us feels that we would be better to head for Fury Beach. The ice hereabouts held us tight last year. Another year here and we'll all be dead."

Many of the men around me were nodding.

"I understand your concern," Mr. Crozier said, "and we have discussed that possibility. But even if the supplies Ross abandoned at Fury Beach have not been pillaged by natives or whalers, there is nothing fresh that will stop the spread of scurvy. Besides that, we have a duty to perform and it is still within our means to perform it. We shall return to the ships and sail on."

Bill looked as if he was about to say more, but Davy stepped forward and said something in his ear. I was close enough to hear, "Now's not the time."

"We have much to do," Mr. Crozier continued. "As you know, the ships' boats have been built onto sleds. We'll use them to ferry the supplies ashore. Once that is complete we shall head south."

The meeting broke up with much mumbled discussion. However, everyone set to with a will, and for several days, lines of sleds ferried supplies over to Victory Point. Every day the hours of daylight increased and the weather held fair. The work of dragging the heavy, laden boats was so brutal that a number of men collapsed and could do nothing other than stumble over the ice to the island camp.

Before I fell into exhausted slumber each night, I wondered how our weakened crews would manage on the long trek south to Back's Fish River, especially if the weather deteriorated, as was almost inevitable this early in the year. The good sign was that, with the hard work, the grumbling about Fury Beach ceased. On April 25, all was ready. Mr. Crozier had Lieutenant Irving go to the cairn where Mr. Gore had deposited the brief note the year before. Mr. Fitzjames added a second note of our intentions in the margins, and it was reburied. The following day we set off south.

We dragged three laden boats, each taking twenty of the fittest men to haul and push. The remainder dragged light sleds or stumbled along as best they could. We were fortunate in three ways: the landscape of King William Island was flat, the ground remained frozen and snow covered, and we were blessed with moderate weather, the mercury rising almost to freezing on occasion. Even so, by the time we reached the south shore of the island, eight more men were dead, and so many were suffering from exhaustion that we could only advance one sled at a time before returning for the next. It was with great relief that we established our large camp on the flat shores of a place we named Franklin Bay.

Our camp, spread along a low ridge that curved around the bay, consisted of four small tents for officers, one cook tent, another for the marines, and two large barrack tents for the men, plus a large hospital tent where surgeons Stanley and Peddie cared for the thirty or so sick or injured men. The tents were rough and ready, sewn together from the canvas we had on board, but what storms plagued us were of short duration and nowhere near as fierce as the one that had doomed the exploration parties a year before.

As soon as we were established, Mr. Crozier sent out hunting parties along the shores of the island and across the frozen strait to the mainland. At first they had little luck, but as May wore on, birds began to appear. We all took heart when Oonalee, his family and several other parties arrived and begin trading. Mr. Fitzjames insisted they camp some distance away so as to avoid a repetition of last year's unfortunate events. If the locals were here, that must mean that game could not be far away. I traded some nails and trinkets for Davy's knife and returned it to him. I suppose I hoped that my gesture might revive our friendship, but Davy simply accepted it with a grunt.

One morning I woke to a strange sound. It was as if hundreds of people were knocking dry sticks together. As I and my companions in the tent dragged ourselves up into confused wakefulness, a musket shot punctuated the sound. That got us moving and we piled out of the tent to see an unforgettable scene.

It was midnight, but as bright as noon. Oonalee and his companions were running in every direction and our own officers were charging forward with muskets raised. But it was not a conflict between people that was occurring. The landscape behind our tent city was alive. Almost as far as I could see was a solid wave of moving, snorting, coughing life. Steam rose in wraithlike clouds from countless puffing nostrils, and heads tossed back and forth. The noise that had woken me was the sound of thousands of antlers knocking against one another as a vast herd of deer moved over the land.

Some men were firing into the herd to no

apparent effect, but Oonalee soon began to get the marines and officers organized. Small groups of Esquimaux ran at the deer, causing a few panicked animals to split off from the main body. These were then dispatched by our muskets. The rest of us were soon pressed into service as butchers.

It was tiring, bloody work, but carried out with smiles and laughter at the incredible bounty we were being offered. Oonalee and the others rushed about with broad grins plastered on their faces. Occasionally, they stopped beside a kill, reached down to rip out a steaming liver, and devoured it with obvious relish, before returning with shouts of laughter to the fray.

The hunt lasted three days, but never at the frantic pace of that first night. We worked hard and gorged ourselves on fresh meat. At last the blood-soaked landscape, like the aftermath of some titanic battle, fell quiet. The deer were gone and the meat stored in frozen pits in the ground. All around, women and children busily scraped the skins and spread them out to dry.

Then our bounty continued. As May turned to June, the birds increased in number. Great flocks of ducks, geese and swans fell to our guns and joined the deer meat in the pits. Eventually, with many expressions of undying friendship on both sides, Oonalee and his companions, their sleds laden with frozen meat and gifts, bade us farewell and headed east along the shore.

Hope was restored and we were happy for the first time in many weeks. Fresh food had defeated the dreaded scurvy, sick men recovered and the hospital tent was near empty. We enjoyed 24 hours of daylight, seemingly limitless supplies of food, and moderate weather. Out in the strait the ice creaked and groaned, and snaking leads of choppy water opened and closed at the whims of wind and tide. It seemed as if, after all we had suffered, we were saved and would soon be on our way through the final stretch of the Passage and heading for home. But like all else in this land, it was a false hope, containing the bitter seeds of our final destruction.

Chapter 13
Mutiny
Franklin Bay, 1848

"Mr. Fitzjames says we will soon be heading back to the ships," I said to Davy as we sat atop a ridge looking over the moving ice in the strait. Our bounty had improved everyone's mood and even old Bill had ceased his griping.

Davy took a long time to answer. "Don't be so sure," he said softly.

"What do you mean? We can't stay here."

"Why not?" Davy asked. He looked at my shocked face and, before I could think of anything to say, went on. "Not over winter, although if any of us're still in this land come the snow, it won't make no difference where we are. Some of the boys are thinking we should stay here a while. We have food aplenty and the hunting's good, and it'll be better when the deer return. A few more weeks here and we'll be as fit as fiddles."

"Then what?"

"Then we head northeast to Fury Beach."

"But that's *hundreds* of miles!" I said.

"Why not? There's supplies there and a good chance of rescue — better than here anyways." I opened my mouth to say something, but Davy held up his hand. "And we'll have the ships' boats. If no one comes to rescue us, we can sail back out of Lancaster Sound."

It sounded simple, and I had to admit that I had thought of something similar, but the decision to return to the ships had been made. "Too much can go wrong," I pointed out. "What if the deer don't return? We have a lot of meat stored, but how long will it last a hundred hungry men? What if the supplies at Fury Beach have been plundered by natives or whalers? What if a storm catches everyone in the open? What if you arrive too late for whalers or a rescue ship to find you at Fury Beach? The three boats can't hold everyone."

"What if. What if. What if." Anger flashed across Davy's face. "What if the ice don't release the ships this year, same as last? Then we'll all die comfy in our hammocks. If I'm to die, I'd rather die on my feet, struggling to save myself, and there's many feel the same. We've had enough of the officers telling us what to do. That's what got us into this mess in the first place."

I wanted to argue that a return to the ships made more sense — that all the signs were that this summer would be milder than last. I wanted to say that we would be safer in the ships and home sooner, but Davy's anger frightened me. What if others felt as strongly as he did? The decision was already made. How would the crews react? I sat in silence.

"You got to choose, Georgie boy," Davy said, "between your mates and them fancy officers you seem so fond of." He stood and headed back to the tents, turning to tell me, "There ain't much time to think on it."

I sat for a long time in an agony of indecision. Who was right? Go back to the ships or head for Fury Beach? Mr. Crozier and the other officers had made a decision and Mr. Fitzjames had told me it would be announced this afternoon.

Some hours later Mr. Crozier, Mr. Fitzjames and the other officers stood in a line on the rise above the beach. The rest of us were spread out on the flat stony area between them and the strait, where lines of open water twisted through the gleaming ice. A cold wind blew from the north, flapping the canvas of the tents, but the sun was bright in a pale blue sky.

"Our journey down here was hard, but it was the right choice," Mr. Crozier said. "We have been fortunate with the hunting and the scurvy has been kept at bay. However, if we are to complete our task this year, it is time to return to the ships. We shall travel light, carrying as much food and essential supplies as we can. The rest we will store here."

Mr. Crozier hesitated, as if he was not comfortable with what he was about to say next. "Surgeon Stanley informs me that about a dozen men are still not fit to travel. He has volunteered to remain here and care for them." A grumble ran through the crowd around me. No one liked the idea of leaving their mates behind.

"I share your concern." Mr. Crozier raised his voice above the discontent. "It goes against all I believe in to split the company this way and leave men behind, but I can see no alternative. They have ample food and the weather remains moderate. As soon as the ships are free of the ice, we shall sail south and reunite the two parties before continuing to warmer climes."

I looked at Mr. Fitzjames. His usual smile was gone and he looked grim. I wondered if he agreed with Mr. Crozier's decision.

"Speed is of the essence if we are to take maximum advantage of what seems to be a mild summer. Let us get to work." Mr. Crozier turned away.

"We ain't going." A voice rang out from the

crowd of sailors beside me. Mr. Crozier turned and scanned the crew. Old Bill stepped forward. "Some of us been talking," he continued, "and we reckon that staying here to hunt more and then heading north to Fury Beach makes more sense."

"Oh, you do, do you?" Mr. Crozier snapped. "And who might 'some of us' be?"

"A good number," Bill said, but he seemed uncertain.

"A good number," Mr. Crozier repeated. "Well, if that 'good number' remain silent, then there will be no need for a good number of floggings. You" — he stared at Bill — "we shall attend to when we return to the ships."

Bill appeared to shrink. He looked around at his companions.

The only one to move was Davy. Cursing under his breath, he stepped forward. Instead of addressing Mr. Crozier, he turned to the group of sailors. "You fear flogging?" he shouted. "You'd rather a lingering death of scurvy and starvation? Because that's what awaits each and every one of us who returns to the ships. You saw the ice last year." Heads began to nod in agreement.

"Ice cliffs as high as the dome of St. Paul's Cathedral," Davy went on, "and moving. Pressure that can reduce a ship to matchwood. Ridges that take a dozen fit men hours to climb with the lightest sled. D'you really think that'll all magically vanish and allow us to go on our merry way?"

He paused. More heads were nodding agreement now.

"That ice river has held our ships imprisoned for two winters and a summer," he continued. "It ain't about to let us go. By the time these officers realize that, it'll be too late. Too late for the men we're abandoning here and too late for us. The ships're a death trap. Our fancy coffins is all they are."

Men were now openly shouting agreement with Davy. Mr. Crozier tried to say something, but no one listened. He spoke to Mr. Fitzjames, who moved over to one side.

Davy didn't back down. "I'll not abandon our mates in the sick tent. I aim to join them now, and when they're fed and fit once more, I'll lead them to Fury Beach, rescue and home. Who's with me?"

The shouting swelled.

"Then follow me," Davy yelled as he moved towards the hospital tent.

Bill and a large group of seamen surged after him. Several others, as if drawn by the weight of the group, followed more hesitantly. Most were able seamen, but I noticed a couple of marines and several petty officers.

In the blink of an eye, the great expedition had fallen apart. The fourteen surviving senior officers stood on the highest point of the ridge. The mutineers, about thirty in number as far as I could tell, clustered sullenly on the high ground around the hospital tent, and the rest of us stood on the beach. A few hovered uncertainly between.

Mr. Fitzjames broke the silence. "Sergeant Bryant, to me." The marine sergeant from *Erebus*, plus Corporal Paterson, Healey and the other marines, trotted over to Mr. Fitzjames. All were dressed in full uniform and each carried a musket. In addition to those from *Erebus*, they were joined by two men from *Terror*, both of whom were jeered by their companions near the hospital tent.

In what was obviously a planned move, Bryant arranged his men in a line facing Davy and the others. They kept their muskets by their sides, but the move was obviously threatening. Most of the undecided men in the middle scuttled back to where I stood.

The silence was heavy and I could hardly believe what was happening. The only Europeans for hundreds of miles were preparing to fight *each other*.

"So you'd kill your own men," Davy cried to

Mr. Fitzjames. "That's all I'd expect from *officers*." He spat the last word. "Well then, I for one ain't afraid." He threw open his jacket and bared his chest. "Shoot me. It will be a quicker, cleaner end than what you offer us back at the ships."

Mr. Fitzjames looked at Mr. Crozier, who nodded. "Sergeant Bryant," Mr. Fitzjames said.

"Make ready," Bryant ordered. His clear voice swept through the cold air. Everyone stood like statues as the marines lifted their muskets. "Present." Muskets were brought up to shoulders and aimed. Several men behind Davy shuffled nervously as the sharp sound of the muskets being cocked rang out.

"Don't worry," Davy said to the crew nearest him. "There's but eight of 'em. They'll get me for sure and maybe a couple more, but there's thirty of you. Move at the sound of the musket's crack. You'll be on 'em afore they can reload." He looked over at Mr. Fitzjames and the others. "Then it'll be the officers' turn."

I blinked and shook my head, unable to believe what I was seeing and hearing. Was Davy really leading a mutiny? Were the marines prepared to fire on comrades who had been through so much with them? The moment seemed to last for an eternity.

"What is this insanity?" Surgeon Stanley shouted. He did not have the rough appearance of those who had spent lives aboard ship, but he was respected and he had volunteered to stay behind with the sick men. His sudden appearance from the hospital tent into the midst of the mutineers focused everyone's attention on him. "Would we kill each other in this remote land? Will that get us home faster? We are not savages. We are civilized men. If we cannot resolve this without bloodshed, we are not worthy of this great undertaking, nor do we deserve to ever see home again."

He moved to the centre of the triangle formed by the three groups of men. His voice wasn't nearly as loud as Sergeant Bryant's or Mr. Crozier's, but everyone was listening. "I propose a compromise." He looked at Mr. Crozier, who, after a moment's reflection, nodded for him to continue.

"I am remaining here with the twelve men too sick to travel. I see no reason why that number could not be increased. I could use the assistance both in caring for the sick and in hunting to increase our food cache. I propose that, as long as enough men decide to return to the ships to sail them down here once the ice frees them, then those who wish to stay and work here be allowed to do so."

"There will have to be an accounting for the events of this day," Mr. Crozier said.

"Indeed there will," Surgeon Stanley agreed, "but can it not wait until we are safe on our journey home? Is that not better than blood staining this barren land?" He turned and looked at Davy, who hesitated for a long moment before nodding slowly.

"Very well," Mr. Crozier said. "Sergeant Bryant, stand your men down. Mr. Fitzjames, organize lists of who will stay and who will return, and begin the packing."

Everyone let out a sigh of relief before excited conversations broke out everywhere. Several men patted Davy on the back, but he ignored them and wandered off alone. I pushed through the crowd to reach him.

"What have you done?" I asked.

"I have saved some of our lives," he replied.

"Are you sure?"

Davy spun to face me. "No. I am not sure. Perhaps we're all doomed. But I am certain that, if all return to the ships, none will survive the coming winter. You saw that ice, Georgie. D'you believe in the depths of your heart that it'll release the ships to sail happily onward?"

I shrugged. I honestly didn't know.

"Of course it won't," Davy said. "Our only hope is Fury Beach."

"Would you really have led an attack on the marines and officers if Surgeon Stanley had not intervened?"

"If those men had fired upon us, yes." Davy gazed out to sea. "I've spent my whole life with people telling me what I can't do — the Beadle in the workhouse, the Peelers on the streets. Mostly I've ignored them or done something different, but this time I ain't got no choice. It's like that time in the churchyard with Jim. I had to attend to him or he'd have done for you, and you're the truest friend I've ever had. It were either stand up to them officers or die on the ships."

Davy fell silent and stared at the ground. I was stunned that, after everything we had been through, he still regarded me as a friend. I wondered if I had failed him. Should I have stood by him more?

Before I could say anything, he continued. "I'm glad Stanley spoke up to prevent bloodshed, but that don't change nothing. Soon as the sick men are fit enough to travel, we'll head for Fury Beach, regardless of what Stanley says." He looked up at me, his eyes pleading. "Will you come with us?"

I almost said yes. It would take a miracle for the

ice to release us early enough in the summer to escape into the Pacific before we were once more beset, but the lure of the ships and their security, false though it might be, was strong. I felt I had let Davy down by not being the friend he thought I was, and the trek to Fury Beach might be the salvation of us all. But I felt a loyalty to Mr. Fitzjames. He had taught me much over the past three years with patience and good nature. But more than that, in telling me of the struggles he had endured and how he had overcome them, he had shown me what was possible.

I needn't be a clerk in a warehouse in Woolwich. I could be anything I wanted — both Mr. Fitzjames and Davy had shown me that. But what did *I* want? Mr. Fitzjames had lived a life of hard work and discipline and had achieved much. Davy had fought hardship and adversity to be free, to do what he wanted without restriction. Which road did I want to travel? It was time to decide. It was difficult, but I suspected that deep down inside I had always known the answer.

I shook my head. "I must return to the ships."

Davy nodded. "You were always in tighter with the officers than me," he said with a smile. "And who can say which of us is right. I may be, and still end up swinging from a rope. You may sail home free while I starve in this land. I wish you luck, Georgie boy." Davy held out his hand.

"And I you, Davy." I took his hand and we shook. In that instant, we were once more the friends who'd sat by the river and told each other stories.

I turned away. "Wait," Davy said. He pulled his knife from his belt and offered it to me. "You might have use of this."

"But this is your most treasured possession," I said.

Davy shrugged. "It saved your life once. Maybe it will again. Now take it," he ordered with a smile, "else I'll have to give it to Bill and he'll only use it to pick his teeth."

I took the knife. "Thank you," I said, but Davy had already turned away and stepped over to join Bill.

"Well, Bill," he said to his old friend, "the die is cast. We'd best make a go of it."

I headed over to where Mr. Fitzjames was organizing several officers to take names and begin stocking supplies for the journey back to the ships. He saw me coming and beckoned me over. "So your young friend was trying to persuade you to accompany him?" he asked.

"He was, sir," I answered, "but I shall return to the ships."

As we walked, Mr. Fitzjames was moving away from the other officers. "George," he said. "I do not know which path is the right one. If I am honest, I suspect that your friend is correct, and I admire him for saying so, although I can never condone mutiny against authority. I have spoken long with Mr. Crozier and we have covered every possible avenue of escape. He has decided that a return to the ships is our best chance and he is in command. I shall do my utmost to support him as my superior officer."

I wondered if that would have extended to ordering the marines to open fire on the mutineers. I was glad I hadn't found out.

"You have done well over the past years," Mr. Fitzjames continued. "I believe you have a bright future and I will happily support your advancement in the Navy should we both come out of this unscathed. However, should you feel that your chances lie better with your companion at Fury Beach, I will release you from any obligation to me and I will not hold any decision you make against you."

"Thank you," I said, overwhelmed by Mr. Fitzjames's generosity. "I have made my decision. I shall come with you back to the ships."

"Thank you," Mr. Fitzjames said, patting me on

the shoulder. "I appreciate your decision and pray it is the right one. Now, we have much to do if we are to leave as promptly as Mr. Crozier wishes."

Chapter 14
Davy

King William Island, 1848

Fifty-five of us set off to return to the ships — thirteen officers, thirty-four sailors and eight marines. We left behind forty-two at Franklin Bay — Goodsir volunteered to stay and help Stanley, so there were two officers, thirty-eight sailors and two marines. In truth, we left forty-three. My last image of leaving Stanley's camp was of Neptune, sitting outside the tent and watching me toil north. He had a sad look in his eyes, but he had decided to stay with the food. I wondered if he was smarter than me.

We travelled light, but the lack of snow on the ridges forced us to drag our sleds on the sea ice close to shore. It was a struggle, continually slipping and often wading knee-deep for hours through icy water and slush. Surgeon Peddie was kept busy with his knife removing frost-blackened toes.

The *Terror* was so badly damaged and we were so few that we only manned *Erebus*. Mr. Crozier took command as we waited for release. The weather was mild and the ice much more active than the previous summer, raising our hopes for liberation. Even fixed in the ice, the ships had drifted south so that Victory Point rather than Cape Felix was now our closest landfall. The active ice encouraged us, but the movement that might release us was also treacherous.

Lieutenant Irving was in a long boat with four sailors, directing the movement of what we could salvage from *Terror*. The boat was in a narrow lead and the ice on one side was old, thick and piled in vast tilted pressure peaks. With no warning, a deafening roar sounded and the ice lurched sickeningly. A great block fell to the water, catching the stern of Irving's boat and crushing it. Water and spray surged up, and when it cleared the boat, Mr. Irving and the four sailors were gone. We found only Mr. Irving's body drifting in the lead, and buried him at Victory Point. Another grave.

Week after week we worked our way south at the mercy of the moving ice and what leads opened for us. As the shores of King William Island became merely a slightly darker line on the horizon, concern mounted over the party left at Franklin Bay. Several attempts were made to make contact, but all were turned back by the treacherous condition of the ice. As August turned to September and the days shortened, we were engulfed in impenetrable fog for days on end. Then the winds from the north returned, blowing the fog away, but bringing snow and cold. Leads closed or froze over and our supply of food dwindled.

We still had barrels of flour for making biscuits, although we had to chop wood from the wreck of *Terror* to fuel Richard Wall's stove. We had tea, chocolate and sugar and enough salt pork for a half pound every second day for each man, but the deer meat from Franklin Bay and the lemon juice were gone. By October, scurvy had returned. At the first reappearance of the disease, Mr. Crozier judged that the ice was stable enough to attempt a journey to Franklin Bay and ordered Mr. Fitzjames to undertake it.

"You must let me come," I insisted as Mr. Fitzjames prepared to leave.

"You will be safer on the ships," he said, without much enthusiasm. He was sitting in the Great Cabin writing instructions for those who would stay behind. "You know what travel is like under these conditions."

"I do," I said, remembering the journey to look for Mr. Gore's party, "but I think any hardship would be preferable to being trapped here on the ship. Besides, Davy's at Franklin Bay."

Mr. Fitzjames laid his quill down and looked up at me. He was not the cheerful, optimistic man I had known at the beginning of the voyage. Like all of us, he had lost weight and his clothes hung from his frame. His eyes were sunken and he had forgotten how to smile. "I would give an arm not to go to Franklin Bay," he said, his voice quiet.

"But we must try to help them," I said, shocked at his attitude.

"Indeed we must," he agreed. "But I awake at night in terror of what we may find there."

"They will have suffered," I said, "but the only casualties we have suffered were in an accident."

"Of course," he said, making an effort to sound positive, "and you must indeed come with us to help your friend."

We set off, two sleds hauled by eight men each, one led by Mr. Fitzjames, the other by Mr. Le Vesconte. A third sled accompanied us as far as the shore. Its purpose was to set up a supply cache on the shore before returning to the ship. The journey over the ice to King William Island took three days, much of the travel in darkness. We set up our land camp on the north shore of the wide peninsula that separated us from Franklin Bay, planning to rest for a few hours before continuing. I was increasingly scared of what we might find at Franklin Bay, but the horror came sooner than I expected.

We were melting snow over our tiny oil stoves when Davy staggered out of the darkness. At first I didn't recognize the shapeless figure stumbling towards us and thought it was some kind of animal. Even when we exposed his face, it was so blackened by frostbite and dirt that it took a moment to see who it was.

Davy was delirious, his eyes unable to focus and flitting from one of our shadowy forms to another. Despite our desperate questioning, we could get no sense out of him. All that was intelligible was a few disconnected words and the phrase, "They're after me," which he repeated over and over, his voice shaking every time.

"We shall continue as planned tomorrow," Mr. Fitzjames said eventually. "We can get nothing at present from this poor wretch. Place him on the sled and take him back to the ship. God willing, he will recover with a bit of care and warmth.

"Young George," he added, addressing me. "You will take Able Seaman Strong's place on the returning sled."

I was grateful for the chance to accompany Davy back to the ships, but horrified at his condition. And if he was this bad, what were conditions at Franklin Bay like?

Throughout our journey back to *Erebus* and for two days after, Davy rambled incoherently and drifted in and out of consciousness. Surgeon Peddie removed most of his toes and several fingers that were so frostbitten that they were beginning to rot. Other than that he could do little but keep Davy comfortable and try to force some warm soup down his throat.

I spent most of my time with Davy, who had been placed in one of the officers' empty cabins, as the sick bay was full. I tried to spoon-feed him soup and tea, replaced his blankets when he threw them off and talked gently to him when he went into one of his frequent fits of panic. At those times he thrashed around, shouting about being chased by ghosts.

On the second day, Davy calmed down and fell into a deep sleep. I was worried that he was dying, but he looked relaxed and I drifted into an exhausted sleep beside him.

"Georgie boy."

I woke to Davy sitting up in his bunk and prodding me with his bandaged hands. "Where am I?"

"Aboard *Erebus*," I replied. "Two days past, we

found you wandering and brought you here. How are you feeling?"

Davy ignored my question. He was still horribly pale and his eyes tended to drift away from me as he spoke, but he was more aware of his surroundings than he'd been since we found him. "Have you been to the camp?"

"No."

"Thank God."

"Mr. Fitzjames is leading a party there now to help."

"No! No! No! He must not." Davy became suddenly very agitated.

"It's all right," I said, trying to soothe him. "He will help whoever's there."

Davy stared at me for a long moment. His eyes were wide and his whole body tense, his bandaged hands held out in front of him. Then, suddenly, he relaxed. His shoulders sagged and his arms fell by his sides. He began to cry in great shuddering sobs. I put my arm round his shoulders and held him until he quietened. Snuffling loudly, he drew away from me, wiped his eyes and nose on his sleeve and sucked in a long breath. "There's something I have to tell you, Georgie," he said.

"There's no rush," I said. "Rest and wait until Mr. Fitzjames gets back."

Davy shook his head. "I shall never rest again, and I don't know how much time is left. I do not wish to go to the grave carrying the secrets I keep in here." He waved a bandaged hand at his head. "I thought that on the streets of London I'd seen the depths a human being could sink to. I were wrong. Listen to me. I must tell it all. Else I'll have no peace in this world or the next one."

"I'll listen," I promised.

"Thank you," he said. "I hope you will not regret that promise."

"At first we was fine at the camp. The food were plentiful, the weather mild and the sick recovering." Davy's eyes were focused on some distant scene and he spoke in a soft monotone, as if he were simply reciting something rather than telling a story.

I felt, with a shiver, as if I were listening to a ghost from a Gothic tale.

"The deer never came back, but there was plenty of birds. We killed one of them white bears, even bigger'n the one that scared you. D'you remember?" he asked.

"I do. You saved my life."

"D'you still thank me for that? Anyways, we stayed longer'n we should, but some was beginning to sicken with vomiting, pains in the head, fevers and stumbling. Stanley were at a loss and could do nothing other than treat what symptoms he could.

"We argued as to whether we should leave the sick. Some, led by Bill, took what food remained, and left one night for Fury Beach. Don't know what became of them. The sickness spread and we still hesitated — couldn't abandon our comrades, I reckon. Even those not sick did nothing. It was as if they'd died already, but were still walking around. Then the cold came and the sick started to die.

"Fourteen of us — the fittest — decided to drag a boat back north, and find you. We took little enough — some biscuits and chocolate — the fresh food were all gone, the animals long vanished and scurvy were back amongst us.

"The weather, exhaustion and sickness stopped us. I don't know how long we huddled in the boat, but it were long days of darkness and horror. Those that died, we pushed out into the snow, all the while wondering who'd be next."

Davy fell silent. His gaze remained distant and I could think of nothing that might encourage him to continue. I waited patiently, certain that the climax of his tale was coming.

Eventually his eyes flicked round to stare at me.

They were wild. He pawed at me ineffectually with the bandaged stumps of his hands. "I'm going to Hell," he said.

I tried to argue with him, but he shook his head, took a deep breath and continued. "Only two of us, me and Johnny, were left alive. I said we should march out to search for the ships. Better to die on the ice than linger in the boat. But we were too weak. We needed to eat to build our strength."

Once more Davy fell silent. His brow furrowed, his eyes widened and his breath came harsh through clenched teeth.

"You did the right thing," I offered.

"Hah!" Davy shouted. "The right thing! What can you, a pampered officer's pet, know of the right thing, or of what Johnny and I talked of and decided upon in that horror boat surrounded by the bodies of our comrades? We gorged, but not on chocolate and biscuits."

As the realization of what Davy had done dawned on me, I felt my eyes go wide.

He nodded. "It were too much for Johnny. He thought the sick men from the camp were coming to seek revenge for their comrades. He sat in the prow of the boat with a loaded musket beside him, ready to defend himself against the shadows he imagined were after him. He even brought one of the dead men into the stern of the boat so he could keep an eye on him. Talking did no good. Johnny just waved the musket at me. I left then, walking north, searching for a place to die, I reckon, but I stumbled upon your camp instead. Why do I still live? Does God require me to confess my sins before I die? Well, I done that. The burden is yours now."

The fire faded in Davy's eyes and he fell back on the bunk, his breathing ragged, his face grey.

I went to find Surgeon Peddie, but when we returned, Davy — my friend, my enemy, my companion — was dead.

Chapter 15
Escape
Boothia Felix, 1849

Mr. Fitzjames and Mr. Le Vesconte returned from Franklin Bay, where they had found no one alive. Surgeon Stanley lay frozen amidst the bodies of the sick beneath the collapsed hospital tent. They also found evidence of the horror Davy spoke about. On the return journey, they came upon the boat. The dead lay about, with Johnny's shrivelled corpse still in the prow, a musket across his knees.

That dreadful winter on the ship was a sad roll call of deaths. Mr. Crozier was one of the first. I think he had given up all hope long ago. Mr. Fitzjames, who was now the leader of our sad expedition, gave me Crozier's skin clothing. We had neither the strength nor the will to give him a fitting funeral on land, and so dug a grave in the thick ice.

Healey died soon after, as did Sinclair and our engineer, John Gregory, who had had little to do since we had run out of coal for his steam engine. They were followed by Osmer, who died mouthing the lists of the long-gone supplies we had brought on board.

More deaths followed week by harrowing week. We laid the bodies on the ice — a halo of death around the ship — as we drifted inexorably south. I think none would have survived had Oonalee not arrived in the spring with a sled laden with seal meat.

As soon as the season permitted, Mr. Fitzjames led the twenty or so survivors east. We passed the Franklin Bay camp on the ice, but did not visit. As we travelled we came upon the sad remnants of the men who had tried to escape Franklin Bay. Most had fallen in their tracks. We found Bill alone on a ridge and Mr. Goodsir in a crude grave with a few rocks covering him.

Beside a group of small islands, we came upon one of the ship's boats. It was undamaged, and as the strait was open, eight of our party determined to sail south and try to ascend Back's Fish River. Mr. Fitzjames tried to convince them it was futile, but he did not stop them when they left. The remainder of us moved on, our party diminishing by the day until, by the time we reached the eastern shore of Boothia Felix, only Mr. Fitzjames and I remained.

We headed north as best we could until, a week

ago, we arrived here. It was a good place to camp. A nearby stream gave us fresh water; an overhang gave us shelter for our crude lean-to and a hill from which we could take turns watching for rescue. We had intended to stay only a day or two before moving on, but we found it impossible to motivate ourselves to undertake even the simple task of collecting our meagre belongings and setting off. We lay in the lean-to or struggled up the hill to sit and stare listlessly at the empty horizon.

All we had for food was the disgusting bitter lichen that I scraped off the rocks and soaked in water from the stream. I remembered from the stories in the book of Sir John's first expedition that there was some nutrition in this, but it helped very little and gave us both severe stomach cramps.

One day I forced myself to take our musket and go in search of game. I had little hope of finding anything — we had seen nothing for days — but Mr. Fitzjames was weakening fast and I found it hard to sit and helplessly watch my friend sink lower.

It took me all morning to travel what I guessed was about a mile from our camp. My stomach had been cramping painfully, so I sat by the shore, watching the waves roll in and hoping that the dark clouds building to the west didn't mean snow. As always, the grey horizon was empty, but there seemed to be more patches of white ice on the water than yesterday. Any whaling captain or rescue vessel that still lingered in these waters at this time of year ran the very real risk of being trapped here over winter. They would all be hurrying home.

Maybe one would be slow. I lowered my gaze to the ground before me. The rocks swam in and out of focus. I concentrated, but could not bring them sharp. It didn't matter. The past was still sharp in my mind's eye and that was where I wanted to be.

I thought of home — happy times with my brothers, Father's stories, Mother's Sunday dinner — but I couldn't hold on to anything. Random images of happiness and horror flitted through my mind.

Perhaps I would have sat there forever, sinking ever deeper into the past, had I not gradually become aware of a figure standing a few paces away. When I lifted my head to look at the Esquimaux man, I thought at first that it was Oonalee, come to rescue us one more time, but this man was a stranger. He was short, dressed in the long skin coat and leggings of his people. His hood was back, revealing greased black hair and a broad grin on his round face. I looked around, but he was alone.

The man stared at Davy's knife in my belt. He pointed at it and then himself. He wanted to trade, but what for? I lifted my hand to my mouth and made eating motions. The man nodded. I handed over the knife. He reached into his coat and pulled out a filthy piece of seal meat and offered it. I took the meat. The man nodded again.

I looked at the meat in my hand. I took a bite. Another. As if by magic, the meat was gone and my stomach was calm. Guilt swept over me. I'd never even considered saving some for Mr. Fitzjames. Perhaps I could bargain for some more. Perhaps I could persuade this stranger to take us to his camp. I looked up, but the landscape was empty. The Esquimaux had vanished as if he had never existed. If I had not been able to still taste the meat and feel the seal grease smearing my face and hands, I would have thought his visit was nothing more than one of my vivid dreams. I did not tell Mr. Fitzjames of the meeting.

Chapter 16
The Last Friend
Boothia Felix, 1849

The day after my meeting with the Esquimaux man, I awoke from a vivid dream of a steaming plate of roast beef, gravy, potatoes and carrots. I could still smell the rich meat, and the bread pudding and custard in the bowl beside it, waiting for me to finish the main course. My mouth filled with saliva and my stomach growled in protest. Tears of frustration made tracks down my cheeks. "I cannot go on," I whispered. "What is the point?"

"The point is hope," Mr. Fitzjames said. "Without that we are nothing. We must keep going as long as we have the strength to place one foot before the other. Every step is an action, a tiny hope that, if we can put enough of them together, might save our lives. Do not give up now, George."

Mr. Fitzjames dragged himself painfully out of our crude lean-to. He lifted his telescope to scan the horizon, as he had done every morning since we had reached the east coast of Boothia Felix. He tried to remain cheerful and hide his condition, but I could see how bad he was. His legs were swollen and he could no longer even climb our low hill.

Not that I was in much better condition. The piece of seal meat and some lichen was all I had eaten in days. My stomach cramped and I dreamed of food, yet I was not hungry. The sumptuous banquets I imagined were all in my head. It was as if my mind had decided to stand aside and dispassionately watch as my body consumed itself. I looked at the bones of my joints pushing through my skin like rocks beneath a thin cloth, and wondered vaguely who these strange limbs belonged to.

I crawled out of the lean-to and joined Mr. Fitzjames. He was right; we had to continue. The water rolled in to the beach and slapped mournfully against the rocks, cold, grey and restless. I scanned the shore as Mr. Fitzjames scanned the horizon. That's when I saw it, something long and curved that wasn't a rock. It was old and stained the same colour as the rocks, which was why I hadn't noticed it before. At first I thought it was just an old whale rib, but as I bent to look more closely, I realized it was something else — a barrel stave. In my dazed state, it took me a moment to understand the immense value of what I had discovered. It was a piece of wood. There were other staves scattered along the shoreline — the remains of a cache, or supplies that had washed ashore from some earlier expedition.

"Look," I croaked triumphantly, "we can have a fire."

When I got no response, I turned to see Mr. Fitzjames lying on the shore, his telescope beside him. I forgot the staves and stumbled over to him. He was barely conscious, his eyes wandering, yet focusing on nothing. I shook him but got no response. I shoved my hands under his shoulders and dragged him back to our shelter. He weighed next to nothing, yet the effort forced me to stop every couple of steps and I collapsed into a fit of violent coughing more than once.

I made Mr. Fitzjames as comfortable as I could on our blankets and lay beside him to recover my strength. "You must get better," I mumbled, desperately trying to fight off the dread loneliness that would engulf me if he died.

Eventually I felt recovered enough to collect the barrel staves for a fire. I had gathered the last of them and was wondering whether I should build a fire or wait until evening, when I spotted the deer. It was a mere 100 yards away on the other side of the stream. It was a young one and shouldn't have been here this late in the season. Perhaps it was a straggler, or sick. Whatever the reason for its presence, it stood completely still, watching me.

Slowly, and without taking my eyes off the deer, I dropped to my knees and reached out for the musket lying by the lean-to. I dragged it towards me, then reached into my satchel for a cartridge and percussion cap. I swung my musket round, pulled back the hammer and inserted the cap. Still holding the deer's eye, I bit the end off the cartridge and pushed it into the musket barrel. My hands shook so much that I banged the ramrod against the barrel as I withdrew it and a shiver ran down the deer's flanks at the sound.

"Please don't run away," I whispered to myself as I gently pushed the cartridge until it was set down the barrel. I swung the musket up, cocked the hammer and aimed. The end of the barrel was waving around wildly. The deer was at the limit of my weapon's accuracy. I forced myself to breathe slowly — in . . . out, in . . . out. The barrel steadied. I squeezed the trigger. My ears rang and the deer vanished behind a cloud of smoke.

Incredibly, when the smoke cleared, the deer was still standing there, watching me. In a panic, I grabbed for another cartridge. The satchel spilled and the percussion caps disappeared into the moss covering the ground. I was on the edge of weeping with frustration — so much food, so close. I was about to begin tearing the moss apart, when the deer sank to its knees. It lifted its head to the sky and snorted once before gently lying on its side.

"I got it," I yelled triumphantly to Mr. Fitzjames. I dropped the musket and, with an energy I hadn't known I possessed, splashed across the stream and headed for the fallen deer in a staggering run. I reached it just in time to see its wide eyes glaze over in death. "Thank you," I said.

I reached to my belt for Davy's knife — nothing. I'd exchanged it for the piece of seal meat. I cursed and looked around until I found a sharp, frost-shattered stone. It was hard work, but I eventually sliced the deer's belly open. Steaming in the cold air, the intestines spilled out onto the ground. I lifted the large, warm, red-brown liver, hesitated only a moment, and bit off a mouthful of the raw meat as I had seen the Esquimaux do on the hunt. It tasted strong and slightly metallic, but it slid down my throat easily.

After four or five mouthfuls, I forced myself to stop. If I gorged, my stomach would rebel and I would end up even weaker than before. Clutching the liver to my chest, like some great treasure, I splashed back across the stream to Mr. Fitzjames. I bit off small pieces and fed them to him. He chewed automatically and swallowed. After four or five mouthfuls, his eyes closed and he fell into a quiet sleep.

While Mr. Fitzjames slept, I worked as best I could on the deer's carcass, stopping every so often to eat more liver and drink the icy water from the stream. At last I had managed to tear off five or six ragged chunks of meat that I stuffed into the satchel and transported back to our camp. I now had no doubt about when to build a fire. I piled the precious wood outside the entrance to the lean-to. Very carefully, I pared off a pile of shavings from one of the staves and broke what was left into small pieces, which I piled beside some dry moss and lichen inside a circle of small stones. By the time I was done, there were still a couple of hours of daylight left.

It took me more time to strike enough sparks off my flint to start some of the moss smouldering. Blowing on it gently rewarded me with a few tiny, tentative flames, enough for some of the wood shavings to catch. I nursed my precious fire until I had a respectable blaze, then stared in awe at the magical flames.

I reached out my hands as close as I dared. It was the first time I'd felt real warmth in many long weeks. I took the pieces of meat and placed them around the fire. The sound of the meat sizzling and spitting was wonderful. How could such a simple thing make me so ridiculously happy?

"A fire."

I turned to see Mr. Fitzjames lying on his side, staring out at the blaze.

"Yes," I said, "and we have deer meat as well. I shot it."

He smiled weakly. "What happened?"

"You collapsed," I said. "I dragged you back up here, found some old barrel staves and shot the deer. The meat's cooking." I felt stupidly proud of my accomplishments, even though the simple tasks had taken me a whole day.

I reached out and grabbed a chunk of deer meat from the fire. It was hot and required some juggling, and the outside was charred while the inside was raw, but it tasted wonderful. Even the hot fat running down my chin was a thrill. I tore small pieces off with my teeth and offered them to Mr. Fitzjames. He shook his head.

"You must eat," I said.

"I am past hunger," he said with a weak smile. Perhaps because I was feeling so much better after the triumphs of my day, Mr. Fitzjames's appearance was shocking. When I had first spied him on board *Erebus* at Woolwich, his face had been fleshy and cheerful. Now his cheekbones threatened to burst through his skin, and his eyes were dark-rimmed and sunken. His beard was patchy and his filthy hair straggled over his ears and down his back. When he spoke, his thin lips pulled back over bleeding gums and missing teeth.

"You must go," he told me, pausing to catch a rattling breath between each word. "Head north along the shore. There is still time to find a whaler."

"I will not leave you," I said.

Mr. Fitzjames sighed. "You are stubborn." His gaze drifted away from me and out the door of our shelter. He took a deep breath and seemed to gain strength from it. "Perhaps we were all too stubborn — stubborn and arrogant. This land does not forgive. Either meet it on its own terms, as the natives who live here do, or it will destroy you, as we are destroyed."

He laughed weakly. "We began this adventure measuring time in years. Would our food last for three years or four? Would we make it through the Passage this year or next? Now our great adventure is measured in days. Will our strength last for another day or two? Will rescue come in the next few hours? The world has narrowed from grand ideas of sailing across the world and travelling the

vards of frozen ground. I
ɔ Russia."

Fitzjames had said in

ames," I said. "Con-

nothing. I
stretched
I soon
had
hile

...ked. I didn't have an answer.
...egret coming here. I have been close to
death before. I suppose sooner or later it had to
win. I regret only two things: all the lost years for
those who died, and that no one will ever know
how we struggled and what we achieved. I'm sorry
I brought you to this."

"You did not," I said, my throat tightening. "I
made my own choices. As Davy did. As we all did."

Mr. Fitzjames looked at me, a faint smile on his
thin, blackened lips. "I suppose we did, for better
or for worse; that is all any of us can do. I'm tired."
He closed his eyes and slept.

I crawled into my sleeping sack and stared into
the flames as the last staves were consumed and
the fire died back to glowing embers. Eventually
I fell into a fitful slumber, huddled on the hard
rocks.

The cold seeping up from the frozen ground
and the chilling air above dragged me back from
sleep. I reached out for a piece of meat from

the rocks beside the fire, but foun

hauled myself out of my sack, stood an

cold-stiffened limbs. It was still dark, bu

discovered that the remaining pieces of me

vanished. It must have been taken by foxes w

I slept.

Misery and despair overwhelmed me and my

emotions swung wildly from weeping to cursing

and back again. I should have replaced the meat

in my satchel. I looked around. My satchel had

disappeared as well. It had been soaked in blood

from carrying the raw meat, so the foxes must

have dragged it off, too. The thought of going and

hacking more meat off the deer exhausted me. My

emotions swung over to an unnatural calm.

"The foxes have stolen our meat," I said to Mr.

Fitzjames.

I got no response, so I reached over and shook

him. His head lolled from side to side. His eyes

were open but staring at nothing. My last friend

was dead.

Epilogue

The sun is lowering in the western sky. How long have I been drifting in the past? Long enough to use up the remaining hours of daylight. As I stand up, every joint aches. My legs are numb, so I stamp my feet to encourage my circulation. Even that slight effort makes me break out in a sweat, and cough. I feel dizzy, so I sit on the rock and scan the empty horizon.

I remember how I agonized over my decision not to go with Davy and to return to the ships. Now, knowing that it made no difference, I wonder if there was anything we could have done that would not have led to this sorry end.

The darkening sky is heavy with clouds. The snow is still holding off, but I don't think it will for much longer. There is no wind, but it is noticeably colder than yesterday.

A single large snowflake drifts slowly down in front of me. It spirals and turns through the cold, still air. I don't think I've ever seen anything quite so beautiful, but such beauty cannot last. I hold out my hand and watch the flake melt as it lands on my palm.

Sighing, I take one last look at the grey horizon and begin the long journey back down the hill. I pass the remains of the deer, cross the stream and bid goodnight to Mr. Fitzjames. I crawl into the lean-to and wrap my sleeping sack about me. Outside, more snowflakes drift down. I feel comfortable and warm and sink into a deep sleep. Perhaps tomorrow there will be a ship.

Historical Note

Sir John Franklin's expedition of 1845 was intended to be the pinnacle of nineteenth-century British Arctic exploration. Building on the work of John and James Ross, William Parry, George Back and others, Franklin was to complete the final short, unknown stretch of the Northwest Passage. His was to be a scientific expedition, tasked with studying the land and the sea, and the animals and peoples who inhabited both. Most important were the magnetic studies, which were to provide a vital part of the ongoing study of Earth's magnetic field across the British Empire.

The total loss of the expedition — not one of the 129 officers and men survived, and the two ships have not been found — shocked the Victorians and provided an enduring mystery that still fascinates today. Dozens of expeditions went in search of survivors — and, later, answers. In doing so, they mapped vastly more of the Canadian Arctic than Franklin could ever have managed, and dramatically increased knowledge of these inhospitable lands.

In 1850, search expeditions discovered the first Franklin wintering site on Beechey Island and the graves of Petty Officer John Torrington, Able Seaman John Hartnell and Royal Marine Private William Braine. Oddly, although a cairn, piles of discarded cans, the site of a magnetic camp, traces of shore buildings and the tracks of exploration parties were found, no written message was apparently left there.

The searches continued, driven in large part by Jane Franklin, until in 1859, parties led by Francis McClintock and William Hobson discovered human bones, a ship's boat containing two skeletons, piles of abandoned clothing and supplies and, at Victory Point, the only written record of the Franklin Expedition, in a tin can underneath a cairn originally built in 1830 by James Ross.

The search for answers continues to this day. In the 1980s, Dr. Owen Beattie, Professor of Anthroplogy at the University of Alberta, dug up the remarkably preserved bodies of Torrington, Hartnell and Braine. He carried out autopsies and analyzed samples of flesh for cause of death. All three men had a range of conditions. Pneumonia killed them, probably as a result of them having tuberculosis, which was called consumption in 1845. They also — particularly Torrington — had high levels of lead in their bodies, which Beattie ascribed to the solder sealing the cans containing the preserved food. He postulated that this was the main cause of the disaster.

Beattie's conclusions have recently been questioned, particularly the solder being the source of the lead in the men's bodies. In any case, the situation is not simple. If all the crew had been ingesting lead at the rate of Torrington, Hartnell and Braine, lead poisoning would have killed everyone long before the 105 survivors abandoned ship and left the note at Victory Point in 1848. The bones on King William Island indicate scurvy and cannibalism, so the mystery remains.

In recent years, several searches have been conducted for *Erebus* and *Terror*, but they have not yet been found. Neither has Franklin's grave nor any of the expedition's records.

In the 1860s, Charles Francis Hall lived with the Inuit to the east of King William Island and wrote down any stories he heard about Europeans in the area. The stories suffered from the vagaries of translation, Hall's prejudices and confusion with other expeditions. Nevertheless, they offer some tantalizing hints. The Inuit stories tell of a ship crushed in the ice and driven ashore, and of another abandoned with a large dead man on board. They tell of meeting desperate groups of starving men hauling sleds over the ice, and of the discovery of a camp with many bodies and evidence of cannibalism (at a place that I call Franklin Bay in the story). Most intriguingly, there are tales of small groups of men on Boothia and the Melville Peninsula years after all of Franklin's men were supposed to have died.

The officers on the expedition are quite well known from their letters and other records. Sir John Franklin was considered a very liberal ship's captain for his day and had been a midshipman on *Billy Ruffian* at Trafalgar. He led two overland expeditions down the Coppermine River to Canada's Arctic coast. On the first of these, eleven of his party of twenty died, and Franklin became known as The Man Who Ate His Boots. He later became Lieutenant-Governor of Van Diemen's Land (Tasmania) before being appointed to head his final expedition.

Francis Rawdon Moira Crozier was probably the most experienced polar explorer on the expedition. In 1845 he had recently returned from being second-in-command to James Ross on his epic circumnavigation of Antarctica, and had been to the Arctic with George Back. His previous experience may explain why, in his letters before they sailed, Crozier does not share the almost universal enthusiasm and confidence in the expedition's outcome.

James Fitzjames was an up-and-coming star in the British Navy after undertaking an expedition along the Euphrates River and fighting in the Opium War in China. He was generally thought to be an orphan, but recent research by William Battersby shows that he was in fact the illegitimate son of Sir James Gambier, a diplomat and member of a very prominent aristocratic family. Fitzjames's letters show him to be a very modern man with a great sense of wonder at the world about him, and a wicked sense of humour. On the final voyage, he kept a detailed and very entertaining journal, the first part of which he sent back to England from Greenland in the summer of 1845. The remainder was lost with the expedition.

Of the lower ranks on Franklin's expedition, not much is generally known apart from their names, ages and what little information can be found in their record of Navy service.

George William Chambers's great-great-great-nephew lives in England and has researched his family. He is descended from George's younger sister Ellen. George did grow up at 58 Church Hill, Woolwich; his father, Thomas, may have fought at Trafalgar. His brother Thomas disappears suddenly from the record and George's two younger brothers, Alexander and William, both joined the Navy.

George and Davy would indeed have had a range of duties and have been at the beck and call of almost anyone needing a task done. However, they would have shared their responsibilities to the officers with a number of other servants, most notably three stewards: Captain's Steward Edmund Hoare, Gunroom Steward Richard Aylmore and Subordinate Officers' Steward, John Bridgens. To simplify the cast of characters in *Graves of Ice*, and to ease the development of the relationship between George and Fitzjames, I have omitted the stewards and given the cabin boys a greater responsibility than they might have had. I apologize to the ghosts of Hoare, Aylmore and Bridgens.

William Braine was photographed when Owen Beattie opened his grave. He had a scar on his forehead and rotten teeth, and had been buried with a red scarf over his face. Signs of decay and animal activity suggest that he died some time before he was buried. The most likely explanation for this is that he died some way from the ship, possibly with an exploring party, although this would not have been normal duty for a marine.

Two of Franklin's men were brought home from the North. Lieutenant Irving's body was identified from a medal found in his grave at Victory Point; he is buried in Dean Cemetery in Edinburgh. For many years a skeleton found on the south shore of King William Island was thought to be that of Lieutenant Henry Thomas Dundas Le Vesconte. Recent studies of the bones, when the skeleton was reinterred in the Old Royal Naval College in Greenwich, suggest that this identification is wrong and that the remains are those of Assistant Surgeon Harry Goodsir.

The expedition was given the best technology available in 1845, including complete steam engines to help propel them through the ice. There was a Daguerrotype apparatus on board and Mr. Beard did come aboard *Erebus* to take a series of now-famous images of the officers, including Franklin with the flu and two poses of James Fitzjames.

The Navy carefully catalogued the supplies given to the expedition, including the thousands of cans delivered at the last moment. There *were* over 2000 kilograms of chocolate on board *Erebus*.

Officers' pets were surprisingly common on ships. Fitzjames himself came back from China with a pet leopard, and there was a monkey called Jacko and a dog called Neptune on *Erebus*.

The dock at Greenhithe from which *Erebus* and *Terror* departed on May 19, 1845, and the inn in which John and Jane Franklin stayed the night before, both still exist. As the ships sailed on that May morning in 1845, Jane did not come to the dock, but watched from one of the upstairs windows of the inn.

The note found by William Hobson at Victory Point in 1859 is one of the most intensely examined Arctic documents in existence. Despite this, it is still open to interpretation. It was originally deposited by Graham Gore and his sledging party in late May or early June of 1847 as they travelled towards Cape Herschel. This note was written by Fitzjames; it gives the location of the ships, a brief record of their achievements and concludes, *All Well*.

In this note, Fitzjames wrongly gives the date of wintering at Beechey Island as 1846/47 and not 1845/46. A confusion with dates is a typical early sign of lead poisoning. The note is open to interpretation as well. Depending how you read it, the ships explored Wellington Channel in 1845 or 1846.

In April of the following year, the note was

retrieved from the cairn and a second message written around the margin, also in Fitzjames's hand. It is from this note that we know Sir John died on June 11, 1847, that only 105 of the original 129 remained alive, and that the ships were being deserted. Frustratingly, the note gives no reason for the desertion, or details of what the survivors' intentions were. After Fitzjames completed the note, Crozier signed it and added *and start on tomorrow 26th for Back's Fish River.* Crozier does not state whether the journey south is an attempted escape or a desperate search for fresh food to stem the spread of scurvy.

Undoubtedly, the greatest legacy of the Franklin Expedition was the incredible amount of exploration that was undertaken by the search parties that set out looking for him. They increased European knowledge of the Arctic vastly more than would have been the case had Franklin succeeded in his task.

However, Franklin's men did make significant discoveries before they died. They sailed up Wellington Channel, which no one before had done, and proved Cornwallis to be an island. They probably discovered what is now called Peel Sound (I have them call it Lady Jane Franklin Strait), and confirmed that King William Island was not attached to Boothia. Lieutenant Gore almost certainly completed the last section of the Northwest Passage by travelling overland to Cape Herschel. There must have been countless other discoveries and explorations, but the records of these — at least for now — are lost.

Both Parks Canada and a handful of individual researchers are still scouring the Arctic for remains of the two lost ships, Franklin's grave and any scrap of records that might have been missed. Maybe one day a sunken ship or a grave containing records or diaries will be found on or near King William Island. If so, questions will be answered and a part of the mystery solved. However, after all these years, we can be certain that anything found will pose as many new questions as it answers. There is no danger that Franklin's mystery will be fully solved or that it will cease to capture our imagination.

A daguerrotype of James Fitzjames carrying his telescope was taken aboard Erebus *a few days before the expedition sailed.*

Bodies surround one of Franklin's boats after the men left the ships. The painting is titled They forged the last links with their lives.

This boat plank, presumed to be from one of the small boats used after the crews abandond the ships, was found near Payer Point, King William Island, in 2011.

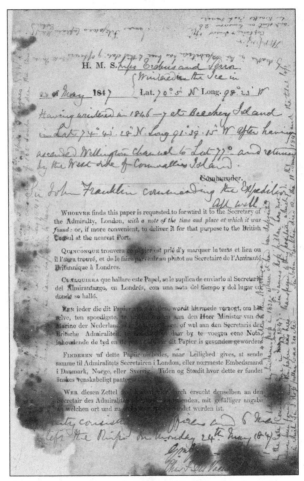

H. M. S.hips *Erebus and Terror*
Wintered in the Ice in

of *May* 184*7* Lat. 70° 5' N Long. 98° 23' W

Having wintered in 1846—7 at Beechey Island

in Lat 74° 43' 28" N. Long 91° 39' 15" W after having

ascended Wellington Channel to Lat 77° and returned

by the West side of Cornwallis Island.

Sir John Franklin *commanding the Expedition.*

All well

WHOEVER finds this paper is requested to forward it to the Secretary of
the Admiralty, London, *with a note of the time and place at which it was
found:* or, if more convenient, to deliver it for that purpose to the British
Consul at the nearest Port.

QUINCONQUE trouvera ce papier est prié d'y marquer le tems et lieu ou
il l'aura trouvé, et de le faire parvenir au plutot au Secretaire de l'Amirauté
Britannique à Londres.

CUALQUIERA que hallare este Papel, se le suplica de enviarlo al Secretario
del Almirantazgo, en Londrés, con una nota del tiempo y del lugar en
donde se halló.

EEN ieder die dit Papier mogt vinden, wordt hiermede verzogt, om het
zelve, ten spoedigste, te willen zenden aan den Heer Minister van de
Marine der Nederlanden in 's Gravenhage, of wel aan den Secretaris der
Britsche Admiraliteit, te London, en daar by te voegen eene Nota,
inhoudende de tyd en de plaats alwaar dit Papier is gevonden geworden

FINDEREN af dette Papiir ombedes, naar Leiligbed gives, at sende
samme til Admiralitets Secretairen i London, eller nærmeste Embedsmand
i Danmark, Norge, eller Sverrig. Tiden og Stædit hvor dette er fundet
ønskes venskabeligt paategnet.

WER diesen Zettel findet, wird hier-durch ersucht denselben an den
Secretair des Admiralitäts in London einzusenden, mit gefälliger angabe
an welchen ort und zu welcher zeit er gefunden worden ist.

Party consisting of... Officers and 6 Men

left the Ships on Monday 24th May 1847

*This message, written in 1847, with notes up the side
added by Fitzjames in 1848, was found by the McClintock
Expedition near Victory Point in 1859.*

This cairn was found on Gore Point, Collinson Inlet. It contained a document similar to the one found by the McClintock Expedition at the Victory Point cairn.

The skull of a European was found by Tom Gross near Booth Point, King William Island. Gross has travelled to the Arctic in search of Franklin artifacts for almost a quarter century.

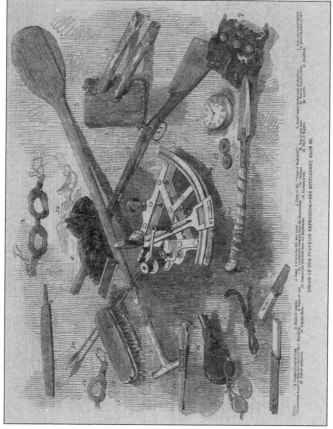

Various items from the 1845 Franklin Expedition include sun goggles, a sextant, a watch, a powder flask and a musket.

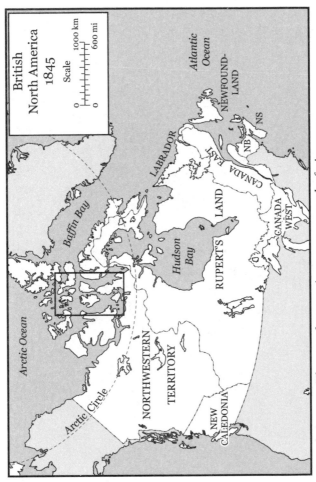

Canada in 1845. The area shown as inset appears on the facing page.

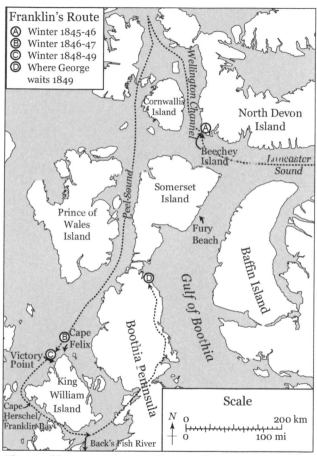

Wellington Channel

Cornwallis
Island

North Devon
Island

Ⓐ

Beechey
Island

Lancaster
Sound

Peel Sound

Somerset
Island

Prince of
Wales
Island

Fury
Beach

Ⓓ

Gulf
of
Boothia

Baffin
Island

Cape
Felix

Ⓑ

Victory
Point Ⓒ

King
William
Island

Boothia Peninsula

Cape
Herschel/
Franklin Bay

Back's Fish River

Scale

N   0   200 km
     0   100 mi

*The possible route of the Franklin Expedition, based on
findings of several search expeditions as well as recorded Inuit
testimony. Peel Sound is called Lady Jane Franklin Strait in
the story.*

Credits

Cover cameo (detail): XAM 79070 *Crown Prince Rudolf*, 1873 (oil on wood) Lenbach, Franz Seraph von (1836-1904) / Wien Museum Karlsplatz, Vienna, Austria / The Bridgeman Art Library.
Cover Scene (detail): *HMS Erebus in the Ice*, © Royal Museums Greenwich, London, BHC3325.
Journal Details: journal © Valentin Agapov/Shutterstock; belly band © ranplett/istockphoto; back cover label © *Thomas Bethge*/Shutterstock.

Page 179: Commander James Fitzjames, © Royal Museums Greenwich, London, 9191B.
Page 180: *They forged the last links with their lives*, © Royal Museums Greenwich, London, BHC1273.
Page 181: Boat plank found near Payer Point, King William Island, NU, © Tom Gross.
Page 182: Message found by the McClintock Expedition near Point Victory, © Royal Museums Greenwich, London, D2184.
Page 183: Gore Point Cairn found in Collinson Inlet, NU, © Tom Gross.
Page 184: Skull found near Booth Point, King William Island, NU, © Tom Gross.
Page 185: Relics of the Franklin Expedition, *Anonyme* – Anonymous, © McCord Museum, M993X.5.1349.2.
Pages 186 and 187: Maps by Paul Heersink/Paperglyphs.

The publisher wishes to thank Janice Weaver for her detailed checking of the facts, and Dr. Russell Potter, editor of *Arctic Book Review*, for sharing his vast expertise about the Franklin expeditions.

Author's Note

The names used in *Graves of Ice* are those of actual crew members on the expedition, although the old sailor Bill is a composite. I have kept to the historical record as closely as possible, but interpreted the known facts in the service of the story. For example, I chose to place the exploration of Wellington Channel in 1846 rather than 1845, which is the common view. The information we have can be interpreted that way and seems to make more sense.

I have seen many of the artifacts brought back by the search expeditions and I have held the Victory Point note. I have visited Lieutenant Irving's grave in Edinburgh and the memorial in Greenwich that contains the remains of Harry Goodsir.

The date given in the text for George's birthday (September 5, 1827) is accurate from family records. This would give his age as 17 when the ships sailed in May 1845, yet he is listed in the Navy muster books as being 18. In fact, three of the four cabin boys are listed as being 18 and the fourth as being 19. This is strangely old for boys in the Navy and seems to contradict the evidence of skeletal remains found in 1993 on King William Island, which belonged to someone who was probably only 14 when the ships sailed. Perhaps some lied about their age.

My interest in the Franklin Expedition was originally triggered by reading the journal fragment that James Fitzjames sent home from Greenland. I liked him and would very much have enjoyed a conversation over a glass of rum punch. As an *homage*, I attempted to recreate the lost journal he kept, as he might have written it. This was published as a novel for adults, *North with Franklin: The Lost Journals of James Fitzjames.*

There are many gaps in the Franklin story into which a novelist can insert his imagination in order to create a plausible tale. I hope those gaps are never closed.

Acknowledgements

A small but dedicated cadre of Franklin enthusiasts have contributed, sometimes without knowing it, to both the historical accuracy and my imaginative fictionalization in *Graves of Ice*.

Russell Potter probably has as broad a knowledge and understanding of Franklin's expedition and its cultural and historical setting as anyone alive. His blog and our e-mailed conversations have been a great help in crafting my tale, as were his comments as historical consultant on the finished document.

William Battersby has researched James Fitzjames's early life and uncovered his true parentage. One afternoon, we sat outside the inn where Sir John and Lady Jane stayed, and speculated which window she had looked out of as her husband sailed into history.

Tom Gross has visited and studied King William Island every summer since the early 1990s, and has probably traversed as much of that land as any European since Franklin's men. Conversations with Tom, as well as seeing his photographs

— some of which he generously allowed me to reproduce here — gave me a sense of why King William Island is not a place you would want to spend a couple of winters.

Tom Swailes, whose great-great-grandmother was George's younger sister, Ellen, kindly gave me permission to use his family research in building George's background.

Dr. Owen Beattie brought Torrington, Hartnell and Braine back to the light of day and allowed us to look on the actual faces of three of Franklin's men.

David Woodman immersed himself in the Inuit testimony collected by Charles Francis Hall and opened up many new avenues of imagination.

Relics from Franklin and his men are on display at the National Maritime Museum in Greenwich, the Scott Polar Research Institute in Cambridge and the Royal Scottish Museum in Edinburgh. The archives of these institutes also contain many letters and documents written by Franklin and his men.

Of course, this novel would not be near as good without the help of the team at Scholastic. In particular, my editor, Sandy Bogart Johnston, tidied up my bad writing habits, reminded me of the reader's perspective and nudged me back to the story when I became sidetracked into some obscure corner of Franklin lore. Janice Weaver did so much research as fact checker that she now qualifies to join the dedicated Franklin brotherhood.

Finally, thanks to my wife, Jenifer, who waited patiently while I visited George's Arctic, even when I was sitting at the dining-room table.

Other books in the I AM CANADA series

Storm the Fortress
The Siege of Quebec
Maxine Trottier

Fire in the Sky
World War I
David Ward

For more information please see the I AM CANADA
website: www.scholastic.ca/iamcanada